'I guess a woman like you… you'd be used to men wanting to impress you.' He flashed her a veiled look. 'Do you receive a lot of offers?'

Not caring to boast, she made a non-committal, so-so sort of gesture. 'Oh, well…'

'I'm not surprised,' he said warmly. 'There are so many of those blokes about. Operators looking for a beautiful woman to hook up with.' He nodded, sighing. 'Yeah, I know the type. First they use the old sweet-talk routine to soften you up. Then they manoeuvre you into a clinch.' He glanced at her, his eyes gleaming. 'Or is that where they start these days? With a kiss?'

As if he didn't know. Her heart bumped into double-time.

This conversation was heading in a certain direction, but it was undeniably thrilling. It had been ages since she'd felt on the verge of something truly dangerous and fantastic. All right, so he was an operator of the worst kind. She could be t                     ln't taken a ce

was she w

D0488473

As a child, **Anna Cleary** loved reading so much that during the midnight hours she was forced to read with a torch under the bedcovers, to lull the suspicions of her sleep-obsessed parents. From an early age she dreamed of writing her own books. She saw herself in a stone cottage by the sea, wearing a velvet smoking jacket and sipping sherry, like Somerset Maugham.

In real life she became a schoolteacher, and her greatest pleasure was teaching children to write beautiful stories.

A little while ago she and one of her friends made a pact to each write the first chapter of a romance novel in their holidays. From writing her very first line Anna was hooked, and she gave up teaching to become a full-time writer. She now lives in Queensland, with a deeply sensitive and intelligent cat. She prefers champagne to sherry, and loves music, books, four-legged people, trees, movies and restaurants.

**Recent titles by the same author:**

**Did you know these are also available as eBooks?**
**Visit www.millsandboon.co.uk**

# KEEPING HER UP ALL NIGHT

BY
ANNA CLEARY

MILLS
BOON

First published in Great Britain 2012
by Mills & Boon, an imprint of Harlequin (UK) Limited.
Harlequin (UK) Limited, Eton House, 18-24 Paradise Road,
Richmond, Surrey TW9 1SR

© Ann Cleary 2012

ISBN: 978 0 263 89315 1

Harlequin (UK) policy is to use papers that are natural, renewable and recyclable products and made from wood grown in sustainable forests. The logging and manufacturing process conform to the legal environmental regulations of the country of origin.

Printed and bound in Spain
by Blackprint CPI, Barcelona

# KEEPING HER UP
# ALL NIGHT

# CHAPTER ONE

GUY WILDER wasn't on the hunt any more. He'd given up chicks with promises of forever on their honeyed tongues. These days he poured his emotions into songs. Often tearjerkers in the key of tragedy, best wailed after midnight in haunts for the broken-hearted. But they were tuneful, sexy, and always with a deep and honest soul beat. Songs a man could believe in, with no bitter twists at the end.

Yep, he was still a single man, and it was all good. By day he built his company, by night he dreamed up songs, and the Blue Suede boys were keen to perform them.

However badly they murdered his lyrics, the Suede showed promise. So, on the night of his return from a work trip to the States, the boys' need for an emergency venue persuaded Guy to let them into his aunt's apartment above the Kirribilli Mansions Arcade. Auntie Jean wouldn't mind. Well, she was trusting *him* to hang there for a week or two.

The thing was, the Suede could pound out a pretty stirring beat. Guy did give *some* consideration to the noise. When the boys crowded through the door with their instruments he eyed the flowery fanlight above the neighbour's place, but the apartment was in darkness.

It wasn't late enough for sleeping. Who'd have guessed anyone was home?

He ordered pizza, but once he and the guys started on the song dinner floated from their minds. It wasn't until the tempo had hotted up and they were into laying down chords that the distant ding of the bell penetrated the boys' enthusiasm.

Calling a halt, Guy abandoned the keyboard of his aunt's fabulous old grand and headed for the door.

The pizza lad was out there, all right, but not at Guy's door. At the neighbour's.

'I assure you it wasn't me,' the woman was saying in a low, melodious voice. 'I never order pizza. It must have been whoever's in there, making that awful racket. Did you try knocking? Though you might need a sledgehammer to make any…'

*Impact.* Guy finished the sentence for her in his head.

She swivelled around to look at him, as did the boy, and impact happened.

Violet eyes, dark-fringed and serious, and cheekbones in a piquant face. A mouth as ripe and sweet as a plum. Gorgeous, was his first dazzled thought. A gorgeous, desirable, tantalising—trap. She was five feet six or thereabouts, unless his expert eye was dazzled out of whack, with long, dark, lustrous hair tied back. Gloriously *rich*, long, dark and lustrous. And legs… Oh, God, legs. And heaven in between.

He couldn't see much of the heaven through the sweatshirt, but all the signs were there. Hills. Valleys. Curves. Anyway, a man didn't stare obviously at a woman's breasts. Or any other parts they might choose to conceal.

But if she happened to be wearing a short flimsy-looking dress thing, frilling out from under the longish sweatshirt, naturally his eye was bound to be snagged here and there. Particularly if she also had satin slippers on her feet. Tied on ballerina fashion, with criss-crossing strings.

He drank her in to the full, and she gave him every reason to believe she was eyeing him right back—only hers was a sternish scrutiny that seemed not to be dwelling on his manly appeal.

He smiled. 'I think they're for me.' He produced money and accepted the pile of boxes. 'Thanks, mate. Keep this for your trouble.'

The lad disappeared via the lift, the stairs—or maybe he vanished through the wall.

'Sorry if you were disturbed, Miss…?'

'Amber O'Neill.' Her tone was earnest. 'I don't think you realise how much the sound reverberates in these apartments. It magnifies, actually, and the walls are very thin.'

He lifted his brows. 'Yeah? The sound magnifies. Now, that's interesting. A unique accoustic. Thanks for mentioning it.'

*Amber*, he was thinking, riveted on her irises, drowning in the violet. And her mouth—so soft and full. A dangerous yearning stirred the devil in his blood. Oh, man, it had been a long, long time.

Apparently she still hadn't noticed his charm, for her luscious lips tightened. 'Some people have to work, you know. Some even have businesses to run.'

'Do they?' He smiled, refusing to be chastised at eight-thirty in the evening. Practically daylight. Enjoying stretching out the tease. Listening to her voice. 'Tsk. Don't those people ever play?'

Maybe he should suggest she throw him over her lap and spank him. Now, there would be an inspiration. And right next door, too.

At the exact moment his brain generated the backsliding thought, he noticed her flick a glowing little glance over his chest and arms and down below his belt buckle. Despite her indignation, her eyes betrayed an infinitesimal spark.

An intensely feminine spark that opened a Pandora's box of frightening possibilities.

*Whoa, there.* The hot rush on its way to his loins faltered and screeched to a halt.

Like a madman he turned back into his flat and shut the door. Stood paralysed, breathing for a dozen thundering heartbeats, before he realised the craziness of the impulse and snatched it open again.

Too late, though. She'd gone.


Breathing hard, Amber stood under the skylight in her empty sitting room and tried to resuscitate the mood.

Once more the ethereal chords of 'Clair de Lune' drifted on the air. Usually every note was a drop of silver magic on her soul, but though she rose on her toes and held up her arms to the moon filtering through the skylight… *arabesque, arabesque, glissé…*

Hopeless. The magic was gone. Murdered.

She switched off the music. She couldn't remember the last time she'd felt so annoyed. No use attempting to dance her insomnia away now. She could still hear the appalling racket from next door, even though they'd toned down the volume a notch. The truth was she didn't want to be aware of them in the slightest. Of *him*.

And it had nothing to do with his mouth, or the way he'd looked in those jeans. She was used to well-built guys with chests. She was up to *here* with them, if the truth be known. And no way was it his eyes. She'd seen plenty of large grey, crinkling-at-the-corners eyes in her twenty-six years.

No, it had been the mockery in them. That amused, ironic assumption that since he was a man and she was a woman she'd be keen. He was so sure of himself he hadn't even bothered to finish the conversation.

How wrong could a man be? The last guy who'd persuaded her to take that plunge had reminded her of all a woman needed to learn about heartbreak.

She peeled off her slippers and crawled back into her bed. For a while she lay on her side, as tense as a wire. Tried the other side. Still no good. Tossed. Turned. And in no time at all her brain was back to its churning.

Money. The shop. The renovations. Aloneness. Men who mocked you with smiling eyes.

Usually by late afternoon, the Fleur Elise end of the Kirribilli Mansions Arcade was quiet. This day, surely one of the longest in Amber's memory, not a shopper stirred. After three disturbed nights Amber welcomed the possibility of snatching a quick reflective snooze in the room where the bouquets were made up.

Unfortunately Ivy, the book-keeper she'd inherited along with the shop, had come in to help out.

'…you're going to have to make cuts. *Amber*? Are you listening?'

Amber winced. It wasn't the first time she'd noticed the penetrating quality of Ivy's voice. With only the mildest exclamation the woman could break windows.

Amber laid her aching head on the bunching table. Sleep deprivation had brought her nerves to a desperate state, thanks to that man. For two days now there'd been this throb in her temples. Maybe if she ignored Ivy she'd shut up.

As far as Amber was concerned this was not the moment to be raking over her failures with the accounts. She was tired. She needed to brood on what was happening in Jean's flat night after night. The noise. The ructions.

That—*guy*. She clenched her teeth. The sooner Jean and Stuart got back from their honeymoon the better.

She so resented the way he'd looked at her, with that scorching glance, that lazy smile playing on his cool, very, very sexy mouth.

Maybe he'd thought she'd be flattered. What men didn't realise was that women *knew* when they weren't looking their best. If a woman was wearing an old sloppy joe over her nightie and a man happened to show a certain kind of interest in her, it wasn't flattering in the least. It immediately raised the likelihood that he automatically looked at every woman like that. In other words, he was likely to be the sort of chronic womaniser her father had been.

Oh, yeah. He looked the type, with that lazy grin. Typical narcissistic heartbreaker. If he saw her today, though, even *he* wouldn't look twice. She was a train wreck.

She rested her head on her arms. One of the songs his band had been bashing out was grinding an unwelcome path through her brain. To add to her irritation, when she'd been bathing this morning she'd heard him in his shower, actually whistling the same tune in a slow, sexy, up-beat sort of way.

Why hadn't Jean warned her? They were friends, weren't they? She was the one who was supposed to be looking after Jean's fish and watering her plants.

It was so unfair. With all she had on her plate, she shouldn't have to be so distracted.

'…cut your overheads.' Ivy's voice hacked through the fog of Amber's musings like a saw-toothed laser. 'That Serena's a prime example.'

Shocked into responding, Amber said hoarsely, 'What? Did you say I should sack *Serena*?'

'Well, unless you cut your expenditure elsewhere.'

Amber was flummoxed. 'Oh, Ivy. Serena's our only genuine florist. Neither of us has her sort of talent. All right, I know she's needed a bit of time off since she had the baby. But when she sorts out childcare that'll get better. She really needs the work. She and the babe depend on her hours here.'

'I'm not running a blessed charity,' Ivy muttered. 'Next you'll be talking again about opening up the side door to the street and spending a fortune on redecorating.'

Amber felt her muscles clench all over. Ivy wasn't running anything. Fleur Elise was *her* shop. *Her* inheritance from *her* mother. The words burned on her tongue but with a supreme effort she held them back. That business course she was studying strongly advocated the need to stay calm in times of conflict. Maintain her cool professionalism.

She drew a long, cooling breath. Several long breaths. She needed to remind herself her mother had had a great deal of faith in Ivy. Ivy's legendary ability to avoid outlay was an asset, her mother had said. And it almost certainly was. Anywhere but a flower shop.

Amber's flower shop, at least. Her shop should be spilling over with blooms. Poppies and tulips, snapdragons and violets, jonquils, forget-me-nots. Masses of everything—and roses, roses, roses. She dreamed of her rich, heady fragrances drawing people in from the street and following them throughout the arcade.

All right, she was the first to admit she might not be quite up to scratch yet as a businessperson—she was still in the early stages of her course—but instinct told her Ivy's miserly cheese-paring approach wasn't the way to go.

What *would* attract the customers was a mass of colours, textures and tantalising smells. The sort that would appeal to any sensuous, voluptuous *femme* like herself.

The self she could be, that was. On a good day. When

she'd had *sleep*. When her brain hadn't been tormented by *noise*. Today her sensuous, voluptuous quotient was at rock-bottom.

It was never any use arguing with Ivy, anyway. Nothing would shift her from her fixed position on any subject. If Amber hadn't been so punch-drunk with fatigue she'd have remembered that and kept her mouth shut. As it was…

'I'm thinking of getting a bank loan.' She yawned.

Oh, wow. *Wrong thing to say.* She'd have been better throwing a grenade. Ivy's short neck could stretch right out and swivel when she was outraged, alarmed and aghast.

Like now.

The small woman's mouth gaped into an incredulous rectangle. 'Are you out of your *mind*, girl? How will you pay it back if something goes wrong with the trade?'

'Oh, what trade?' Amber growled, incensed at being called 'girl'. For God's sake, though she might dress like it, Ivy was hardly her grandmother. She was only thirty-eight.

Amber pressed a couple of cooling roses to her temples. 'Do we have to talk about it now, Ivy?' she moaned. 'I have a headache.'

And she needed to brood. About men and betrayal. Love and pain. Passion unrequited. She wasn't sure why these things had to occupy her mind right now, when she was so tired and noise-battered, but for some reason lately they'd been looming large.

For three nights, in fact. Ever since she'd laid eyes on that—*hoon* next door.

It wasn't that she found him so hot. Oh, all right, he was sexy—in a down-and-dirty, unshaven sort of way. Those jeans he wore should be dumped on the nearest bonfire. And as for that ragged old tee shirt she'd seen him in yesterday morning at the bakery… It looked to her as if someone had tried to claw it off him. Some desperate person.

No, *not* like her at all. She wasn't desperate. She simply had a distinctive personality type that could be deeply affected by the sight of sweat glistening on bronzed, masculine arms. She was a highly sensual woman, with a sensual woman's needs.

Very much the Eustacia Vye type, in fact.

She'd discovered Eustacia yesterday, during a few guilty moments of escapist reading in the shop. Well, there were never any customers at that time. If Ivy hadn't insisted on coming in to help out this afternoon Amber might have had a chance to learn more about her exotic heroine. As it was she'd had to hide the book in her secret cache behind the potted ferns.

Eustacia was a woman so sensuous, so voluptuous, that if ever a dangling bough happened to caress her hair whilst she was rambling under the trees in the Wessex woods, the bewitching creature would turn right back and ramble under them again.

Fine. Amber accepted that she wasn't all that beautiful or bewitching. Unless swathed in tulle and feathers, that was. On stage, illuminated in a pool of magic light. She could be pretty bewitching then. Just stick her in front of the footlights with an orchestra swelling to a crescendo and Amber O'Neill could bewitch the pants off a sphinx.

And her hair craved caresses. Ached for them. Though preferably administered via a lean, masculine hand rather than a twig.

She yawned again. Weren't musicians supposed to have skinny arms and hollow chests?

'Tsk, tsk, tsk, tsk, *tsk*.' Even a tongue click from Ivy could attack the cerebral cortex like an ice-pick. 'Have you been hiding these bills, Amber?'

Amber felt herself getting hot. 'Not *hiding*. I just…may

have…put them aside for a… Look, Ivy, I don't feel like doing this now.'

But Ivy would show no mercy. Once she had her sharp little teeth into something she held on like a terrier until she'd pulled out all the entrails.

She waved a bunch of invoices in front of Amber's face. 'You know what I think? You're going downhill. You'll just have to face it, girl. Your best option is to sell. Do you want to be declared bankrupt?'

The word scrambled Amber's insides like a butter churn.

She tried to breathe. 'Ivy, try to understand. This was Mum's shop. She *loved* this shop.'

But the humourless round eyes beneath Ivy's straight brown fringe were as understanding as two hypodermic syringes. 'Your *mother* managed to pay the bills. Your *mother* knew how to take advice.'

Amber flinched. For a small woman, Ivy could pack a lethal punch. Amber knew very well Lise hadn't always been able to pay the bills. But she wasn't about to argue over her mother's faults or otherwise.

Her mother was in the cold, cold ground. And it scraped Amber's heart every time Ivy dragged her name into the conversation. She couldn't handle it with her loss still so fresh and piercing.

Amber drew a long, simmering breath. Lucky for Ivy, she was ace at controlling her temper. That was one thing she could do well. If left in peace. That was all she really craved now. Peace, and hours and hours of deep, uninterrupted sleep.

Was that so much to ask? Ever since she'd relinquished twirling around on her toes to care for her poor mother, she couldn't seem to find those essential things anywhere.

'Have you seen the price of those long-stemmed roses?'

Ivy carped. 'Why can't you just go for the cheaper produce? Why can't you *ever*...?'

The words prodded Amber's insides like red-hot needles. She held her breath.

'Just look at this item here. Why order freesias out of season? You can't afford them.'

Amber gritted her teeth and said steadily, 'You know Mum loves—*loved* freesias, Ivy. They're—they were her favourites.' Inevitably a lump rose in her throat and her eyes swam. Her voice went all murky. 'It's important to have flowers with fragrance.'

'Fragrance, crap. Fragrance is a luxury we can't afford.'

There were still ten minutes to go before closing. Amber knew Ivy was only trying to teach her the ropes, was doing her best according to her own weird lights, but Amber felt an overpowering need to escape. And quickly. Before she let loose and annihilated the little terrier with a few well-chosen words.

She staggered to her feet. 'I'm sorry, Ivy, I can't deal with all this now. I have a killer migraine. I'm going upstairs. Do you mind locking up?'

Ivy's jaw dropped, then she snapped her sharp little teeth together. Even so, her unspoken words fractured the fragile air like a clarion horn. *Your mother never left early.*

This was hardly true, but why should it matter? Amber wondered drearily. There'd barely been any customers then and there wouldn't be any now.

She shoved her way through the potted ferns and the sparse display of bouquets and made her escape into the arcade before the book-keeper had time to lash her with any more advice. As she stumbled down the arcade to the lifts, past all the other glossy shops, she felt her migraine escalate.

In truth, she was starting to feel slightly sick every time she thought of Fleur Elise.

The ninth floor was blessedly silent. Amber unlocked the door to her flat and was met by a wave of hot, musty air. Resisting the temptation of the air-conditioner, she lurched around opening the windows and balcony doors. Then she tore the pins from her hair and let it fall to her waist. Dragging off her clothes, she collapsed at last onto the bed, her nerves stretched taut as bowstrings.

She closed her eyes. If she'd still been in the ballet company she'd be on the tram now, heading home after a beautiful day of music and extreme exercise, humming Tchaikovsky, her muscles aching, her spirit singing with endorphins.

Would she ever feel like that again in her life?

A frightening thought gripped her by the throat. What if Centre Management acted on their rules? What if next she *lost the shop*?

Fatigued though she was, it seemed like an age before her panic wore itself out. Eventually, though, exhaustion started its work. Her anxiety released its grip, and the pain in her temples lightened a little. A merciful cooling breeze from Sydney Harbour rustled the filmy curtains either side of the balcony doors and whispered over her skin like balm, and she felt herself start to drift down that peaceful river, dozing towards sleep.

She was nearly there, soothed at long last into blissful oblivion, wrapped in sleep's healing mantle, when a heavy crash jarred through the floorboards and straight through her spinal cord. Her eyes sprang open and her jagged nerves wrenched themselves back into red alert.

The sound came from the other side of the wall.

'Oh, for goodness' *sake*.'

Amber leaped up and tore open her wardrobe to drag

out a skirt and the first top she could lay her hands on. There was no time for shoes. In a fury she flew out of her flat to hammer on her neighbour's door.

Her fist halted in mid-crash as the door opened abruptly.

It was him, of course. All six foot two of him. His stubble had progressed, and somehow his lashes seemed blacker too, though his grey eyes still held the same silvery glint. Leaning a powerful shoulder against the frame, he cast another of those long, slow, considering looks over her—like the king of the pride contemplating a plump little wildebeest.

'Well, well. Amber,' he said, in his deep growl of a voice. 'Nice of you to drop by.'

Was he trying to be *funny*? No doubt in his black tee shirt and the artfully scruffy jeans clinging to his bronzed, muscled frame he was exactly the sort of testosterone machine certain women might have enjoyed bouncing a bit of stimulating repartee back and forth with...

She wasn't one of them.

'That noise you're making,' she rasped. 'I'm trying to sleep and it's disturbing me.'

He lifted his black brows. 'At six in the evening? You should get a life, sweetheart.'

He started to close the door, but Amber was quick. She shoved her foot into the space. 'Now, wait a minute. I *have* a life. A busy life. And it's because you've been assaulting Jean's piano...' She shook her head, outraged at the scandal of it. Jean's beautiful Steinway... 'You and your friends with those stupid drums... That's *why* I need to sleep at six in the evening.'

He looked at her for a long, considering moment, his strong brows still raised in disbelief. 'You don't like music?'

*Her?* Whose first steps had been a dance? She clenched

her teeth. 'I like music, mister. When I hear it. I've already asked you politely. Now, if you don't keep your noise down...'

'Ah. Here it comes. The threat.' He tilted his head to one side and made a thorough appraisal of her from head to toe.

The full scorching force of bold masculine interest lasered through the thin fabric of her clothes. She grew conscious that in her rush she'd chosen a close-fitting top with a deep neckline, she wasn't wearing a bra, and her feet were bare. Only with difficulty did she prevent herself from crossing her arms over her breasts.

'I love women who talk tough,' he said, with a lascivious twitch of a black brow. 'What will you do to me?'

Wild words rocketed to her tongue. The frustrations and anxieties she'd been repressing over days seethed inside their cage. She wanted to rip open his arrogant jugular with her teeth and nails, claw at his lean face, draw his insolent blood.

He broke into a laugh and flash of white, even teeth lit his face. 'Don't do it. Why don't you come in and we'll see if we can work something out?'

She drew herself up. 'Look, Mr...' she hissed.

'Guy. Guy Wilder.' His sexy mouth broke into a smile, but she didn't care that it illuminated his rather harsh face like a sunburst and made him handsome.

'Whatever.' Her breath came in short bursts, as if Vesuvius was seething inside her, alive and molten. 'I came here to ask if your band can practise somewhere else. If you can't be more considerate I'll report you to the Residents' Committee.'

Amusement crept into his voice. 'We seem to be getting a bit heated.'

'Does Jean even know you're here?'

At her escalating pitch his black brows made an eloquent upward twitch. 'Not only does my dear aunt know I'm here, she *wants* me to be here. I'll give you her address, all right? You can check up. Set your mind at rest.'

'I know Jean well, and I know she would strongly object to your upsetting her neighbours. She would never have agreed to your setting up your band in here night and day.'

'It isn't here *night and day*.' His quiet, measured tone made a mockery of her emotion. 'I write songs. The band you've been privileged to hear the last couple of nights—in the *early* part of the evening, let me remind you—were unable to use their usual venue. They have a gig coming up so they needed a run-through. That means...'

'I know what it means,' she snapped. 'And it was no privilege. You might as well know now—your band sucks.'

His black eyebrows flew up and his eyes drifted over her in sardonic appreciation. 'I'll make sure I pass your critique on to the guys.'

She could hardly believe she'd said such a rude thing, but it gave her a reckless satisfaction. Even if he was Jean's nephew, he'd made her suffer.

*If* he was. She had some vague recollection of Jean's stories about various family members. There was the brilliant one who wanted to direct movies, the scientist who'd fallen in love on a voyage to Antarctica, the boy whose girlfriend—the love of his life, Jean had said—had stood him up at the altar and run away with a soldier. She couldn't remember any mention of a musician.

The guy moved slightly. Enough for Amber's critical eye to catch a glimpse of the indoor garden Jean kept in her foyer. Shocked by what she saw, she couldn't restrain herself. 'Just *look* at those anthuriums. Jean would be furious if she knew you were letting her precious plants die. Surely she explained her watering system to you?'

He gave a careless shrug. 'She may have said something.'

'And what about her fish?'

'Fish?'

'Don't tell me you haven't been feeding them? That aquarium is Jean's pride and joy.' She glared at him—at the grey eyes alight in his dark unshaven face, his black eyebrows tilted in quizzical amusement. She'd never in all of her twenty-six years wanted so much to do violence to someone.

'I'm not sure how the fish are doing,' he said smoothly. 'Why don't you come inside and check them out? You can take inventory while you're here, in case I've damaged something.'

She caught the sarcasm but didn't allow it to deter her. She pushed past him into Jean's beautiful, immaculate flat and halted in the middle of the sitting room.

Twilight had invaded. Only one lamp was lit, casting a soft apricot glow, but with the skylight in the foyer and the glow from the aquarium it was enough for her to see the damage. Newspapers were thrown carelessly on the coffee table beside a functioning laptop, more scattered on the rug. A sheet of Jean's expensive piano music had been tossed on the floor as well, near to where a couple of her Swedish crystal wine glasses rested against the rumpled sofa.

'Better, don't you think?' The guy's smug, complacent gaze shifted from the disaster scene to connect with hers. 'Some rooms are like some people. Just cry out for a little messing up.'

Words failed Amber. Too late to try resolving this conflict without the use of aggression. This man deserved aggression—he begged for it—and she was in too deep now to pull out.

She snatched up Jean's precious sonata from the floor, then marched over to the aquarium. It was almost annoying to see the tank as tranquil as ever. No bloated bodies floated on its placid surface.

She glanced back and saw him watching her with his thumbs hooked into his belt, a quirk to his mouth. 'You *have* been feeding them, haven't you?' In her aggravation she rolled Jean's sonata—rolled it and rolled it into a tighter and tighter cylinder. 'This was just a ploy to get me in here, wasn't it?'

He spread his hands. 'Aha. You've guessed my master plan.'

She made a sharp, repudiating gesture with the sonata. 'Don't you mock me. I have every right to complain about your noise.'

'Sure you do.'

He moved a couple of steps, so his big, lean body was close. Close enough for her to feel the heat of him. She couldn't step backwards without crashing into the fish tank, so she stood her ground, her heart rate escalating.

His growly voice was deep and smooth as butter. 'All right, I'm sorry to have stirred you up, Amber. I can see you're a woman of strong passions. I think maybe you *are* a bit tired. People get overwrought.' He drew his brows together and looked narrowly at her. *'Amber?* Are you sure that's your name?'

*'What?'*

'I think it should be Indigo. Or Lavender. Your oldies must have been drunk.' Missing her unamused glare, he shrugged. 'Never mind. I accept your apology. How about a drink?'

'I'm not apologising.' Her voice trembled as she lost the final vestiges of control and reasonable behaviour. 'And I don't want a drink. Just *look* what you've done to Jean's lovely home. You have no right to touch her precious piano. You're a—a vandal. I don't want to know you, or see you, or hear any more of your awful, awful *noise*.'

He studied her with a solemn, meditative gaze. But she knew, damn him, it was an act. Underneath he was dying to laugh. At her.

'You're a bit wired up.'

He advanced further, so that his chest was a mere five centimetres from her breasts. She inhaled the clean, male scent of him and sensed something else in him besides laughter. A high-voltage buzz of electricity that charged her own nerves with adrenaline.

'You should calm down.'

His sensual gaze touched her everywhere, caressed her hair, her throat, lingered on her mouth.

'I think I know a way I can help you to relax.'

*'Oh.'* Fury must have overheated her brain, because she lifted Jean's sonata and whacked him across the face with it.

Danger flashed in his eyes like a lightning strike. She watched, aghast, as a thin red line appeared where the rolled up edge of the paper had struck his cheekbone.

*How could she have?*

The universe shuddered to a stop. There was a moment when they both stood paralysed. Then in a quick, shocking movement he caught hold of her arms.

'You need to learn some control,' he said softly, steel in his voice, his eyes.

Her heart took a violent plunge as his hands burned her upper arms. The breath constricted in her throat.

'Let go of me,' she said, trying to sound calm while her thunderous heartbeat slammed into her ribs. She blustered the first thing that came into her head. 'Don't…don't you even *think* of trying to kiss me.'

His brows swept up in surprise, then his rainwater eyes sparkled like diamonds. As if she'd said something funny.

His lashes flickered half the way down. 'Are you sure you really mean that, Amber?'

Knowing her Freudian slip was flashing a bright neon, while her traitorous lips still tingled with… Well, for goodness' sake his lips were the most ravishing pair she'd encountered at close range for months. Her chaste, unkissed mouth was making a purely kneejerk and understandable chemical response.

Then, in an avalanche of bodily betrayal, her nipples joined in. She could feel a definite weakening arousal in them of a warming kind and wouldn't you know it? More arousal, all the way south.

At the exact instant those sensations registered with her a high-voltage, purely sexual flare lit Guy Wilder's eyes.

'Take your hands off me.' His grip slackened at once and she twisted away. 'Thank you.' Rubbing an arm, she hissed, 'There may be women who buckle at the knees when they meet you, Guy Wilder, but I can assure you I'm not one of them.'

The heat intensified in his gleaming gaze. He gave a knowing, sexy laugh. 'If you say so.' He crossed to the foyer in a couple of long strides and held the door wide. 'You'd better run home, little girl, and cool down. The wicked, wicked man might tempt you into doing something you enjoy.'

She brushed past him, racking her brains for a parting gibe. Then, with an insolent smile, she pointed to the angry patch on his cheek. 'Better put something on that.'

He touched the wound with his fingers. A smile curled the edges of his mouth as he retorted softly, 'Be seeing you, sweetheart.'

The door clicked to behind her.

Guy stood like a man who'd just been slammed some-where strange by a tornado. It took some time for his ag-gravated pulse to ease. The fiery little exchange had stirred him in more ways than one.

He whistled. *Whew.* What a spitfire.

Nothing like a tempestuous woman to whip up a man's blood. His creative spirit was zinging. The way she held herself with that straight, proud back. If only he could get her in front of a camera.

He groaned, thinking of the way she'd glided across the room with that lithe, graceful walk. He felt aroused and at the same time amazingly energised, his whole being like an electric rod.

His blood quickened. How long since he'd felt this way?

God, it felt great.

Safe inside her flat, Amber buried her face in her pillow, her mind churning with images of his handsome, taunting face. The things he'd said. The things *she'd* said.

*Run home, little girl.* The sheer arrogance of that. She clenched her teeth and tried to think of a hands-off way to murder the beast. Though with what she'd done so far, maybe hands-*on* would be more fitting. Why had she done such a terrible thing?

She should be wrung with shame, but to be honest she couldn't even feel very sorry. What was wrong with her? To have actually used violence like some wild virago was completely out of character for her. No one who knew her would believe Amber O'Neill, meek and mild as honey-dew, could be capable of behaving with such a lack of restraint.

Well, no one *now*.

She'd once disgraced herself by pouring a glass of beer over Miguel da Vargas's handsome, lying head, but that was ancient history. Blood under the bridge. And he'd deserved it. *This* was all about sleep. If she didn't get some soon she'd have to be locked up to keep the public safe.

She punched her pillow, tossed and turned, but all to no avail. It was no use. She'd acted like a fool and she knew it. What had happened to her resolve to stay calm in a conflict situation? He'd been the one who'd stayed cool, while she...

She writhed to think of how easily he'd wiped the floor with her. *Run home, little girl.*

There had to be a way of salvaging her feminine honour.

Suddenly she froze on her bed of nails. She could hear him. He was in there, singing to himself like a man without a care in the world. *Or...* The thought stung through her agony. A man gloating.

Where was her feminine spirit? Was she just to lie down and take this?

She scrambled off the bed and took a minute or two to whip on a sexy push-up bra and some shoes with heels. She considered changing the rather deep-cut top, then discarded that idea. She didn't want him to think she'd gone to any trouble.

She smoothed down her skirt, ran a brush through her long hair. A little strategic eyeliner, a spray of perfume. Flicked the puff from her compact over her nose. Then, more presentable this time, more together, more *herself*— she took a fortifying swig of Vee juice from the fridge, and sashayed to his door for a second time.

Striding up to the bell, she gave it one imperative ring.

# CHAPTER TWO

GUY WILDER took his leisurely time. When he finally stood framed in the entrance he seemed even more physical than she remembered. More hard-muscled and athletic. He didn't speak, just raised one arrogant black brow.

'Er...' Her mouth dried. She'd underestimated the sheer, overwhelming force of his presence. Bathed in that cool, merciless gaze, she felt her confidence nearly waver.

'Look,' she said, moistening her lips, 'I think we can be adult about this.'

In a long, searing scrutiny his eyes rested on her mouth, then flickered over her, leaving a scorching imprint on her flesh that wasn't altogether unpleasant, to her intense chagrin. He kept her pride toasting on the spit for torturous seconds, then opened the door just wide enough to admit her.

In the sitting room he leaned negligently against Jean's mantel, his bold gaze surveying her with amusement. 'What did you have in mind?'

It was the moment to apologise. She was a gentle person—*too* gentle, some said. Far too willing to accommodate the male beast. *Be more assertive, Amber. Don't be a doormat, Amber.* Those were the sorts of things girlfriends had said to her in the past.

Normally she'd have begged his pardon, flattered him

with a few waves of her lashes and been charmingly apologetic. But not this time. At the sight of him looking so insolently self-assured, his cool, intensely sensuous mouth beginning to curve in a smile, as though enjoying, *relishing* her discomfort, she felt her feminine pride challenged.

'I merely wish to reiterate the point,' she said coldly, 'that the walls in this building are thin. Now your singing is keeping me awake.'

He smiled, eyes lighting and creasing at the corners. 'You know, it concerns me that such a healthy woman—a woman so lithe, so supple and apparently fit…' He put his head on one side, his mouth edging up just the tiniest sensual bit as he wallowed in his contemplation of her body. 'In such *excellent* condition as yourself, should want to spend so much time sleeping. Do you ever do anything active, Amber? Go to the gym? Go clubbing? Dance till dawn?'

The irony of that. When she knocked herself out three mornings a week at dance class, ran a shop, studied, seized on any gigs going to keep the wolf from the door. 'That's none of your concern.'

He lowered his lashes, smiling a little. 'Well, I'm glad you've come to beg forgiveness.'

'In your dreams. O'Neills never beg.'

There was a glint in his eyes. 'No? Do they sing?'

He moved swiftly, and before she could protest grabbed her and pulled her down with him onto the piano seat. She gasped, braced to pull free, until his deep, quiet voice pinned her to the spot with a direct hit.

'Is it music you're allergic to, Amber, or men?'

She gave a dismissive laugh. 'Oh, *what?* Don't be silly. I like—*love* music.' He slid a bronzed arm around her waist and pulled her close against him. She made a token attempt to break away, but his body was all long, lean bone and muscle, iron-hard and impervious to her resistance.

The clean male scent of him, his vibrant masculine warmth, the touch of his hand on her ribs, sent her dizzy senses into spinning confusion. She should have pushed him away, should have got up and walked out, but something held her there. Something about his touch, her excited pulse and wobbly knees. Her pride. Her need to win this game if it killed her.

'What sort do you like?' Up close, his growly voice had an appealing resonance that stroked her inner ear.

'All sorts. Chopin. Tchaikovsky, of course.'

'Oh, of course.' He smiled.

'Don't mock,' she said quickly. 'Everyone's entitled to their own taste.'

'Sure they are. If you prefer to listen to the *dead*.' His breath tickled her ear. His lips were nearly close enough to brush the sensitive organ.

'They might be dead, but their music will live for eternity.' She flicked him a challenging glance. 'Can you say that about yours?'

He looked amused. 'Now you're really going for the jugular.'

A random thought struck her. She *could*, actually. His jugular wasn't so far away. With just a slight lean she could lick his strong bronzed neck and taste his salt. Relish him with her tongue.

Adrenaline must be screwing her brain.

'*Chopin*, of all people.' He continued to scoff, mischief in his eyes. 'Isn't his stuff a bit wishy-washy for you, Amber? A bit...' He made a levelling gesture. 'Flat?'

Of course he would think that. But there was no use pretending she wasn't a total nerd. Even before a firing squad her conscience wouldn't let her deny her true colours. Not with all the ways Chopin's piano works spoke to her. How subtle they were, and poignant. How they wound their way into the warp and weft of her most tender emotions.

'No. Those pieces just—seep into my soul.' She turned to look at him.

Guy met her clear gaze and felt the kind of lurch he should avoid at all costs. He *should*. But there were her eyes…

He heard himself say dreamily, 'You know, you're soft. Such curly lashes. And those sensational eyes…'

Amber felt a giant blush coming on. Unless a new heat-wave was sweeping Sydney.

Perhaps the man needed glasses or was a raving lunatic. She started to say something to that effect, and stopped. His mouth was gravely beautiful, and so close she had to hold her breath. His lips were wide and curled up at the corners, the upper one thin, the lower one fuller, more sensual. Lips made for kissing a woman into a swoon. Some poor hungry woman. Lips that could draw the very soul from that poor hungry, famished woman's…

*For goodness' sake, Amber.* Fatigue must be distorting her perceptions. Just because he had a lean, chiselled jaw and a stunning profile it didn't mean she should forget the male/female reality.

She gave herself a mental slap. Feet on the ground and an eye to the door. That was a woman's survival kit. That was what her mother had always told her, and Lise O'Neill had known better than most. When the going got tough, men disappeared.

Just because Amber had failed chronically to apply her mother's wisdom on certain other crucial occasions it didn't mean she had to fail now. Here was a prime opportunity to start inoculating herself against the cunning wiles of the wolfhound.

She didn't have to be susceptible. She *could* resist.

'Now, let's see, Amber.' At this distance she could almost feel the rumble of his deep voice in his chest. 'Your lips are like cherries, roses and berries.' He studied them appreciatively. 'Although maybe softer, redder and juicier. I guess I'll have to taste them to get that line exactly right…'

She tensed, waiting, pulse racing, but instead of delivering the anticipated kiss, he continued examining her.

'And your eyes…' He paused to inspect them. 'What rhymes with amethyst?'

He rippled a few tunes, then settling on 'Eleanor Rigby', sang softly. *"Amber O'Neill, mouth sweet as wine. And her eyes are like clear am—e—thyst. Never been ki—issed. Amber O'Neill. She's twenty-nine and she goes to bed early to pine opp—or—tun—i—ties mi—issed…"*

He didn't sing the next line, just played it. He didn't have to. She remembered how it went. *'All the…'*

Her heart panged. 'Very funny. It's not even true.'

'Which part?'

'Any of it.' Her breasts quickly rose and fell inside their confining bra. Anyone would be lonely in her situation. Of course she missed her mother every minute of every day. It was only natural. They'd only had each other. After she'd left the ballet company and all her friends there she hadn't had much opportunity to make new ones, apart from people who worked in the mall.

And she knew why he thought she looked twenty-nine. It had to be her clothes. If it had been any of his concern, she might have explained about her work costumes. The only thing wrong with them, apart from being relentlessly floral, was that they weren't all that shiny new.

Oh, this chronic lack of funds was approaching crisis point. There wasn't much more she could do about it—

unless the vintage shop around the corner had a sudden influx of barely worn clothes with flowery patterns.

She was signed up for Saturday night gigs at a Spanish club in Newtown for the next few weeks, though she'd planned to use those earnings for her stock explosion. She hadn't planned on it—the shop must always come first—but maybe she could use some of her show earnings to buy something modern. Some new jeans, maybe? A little jacket?

Then she remembered Serena. She'd promised to give her an advance on her salary in return for an extra Thursday evening. And Serena deserved all the help she could get.

Amber noticed he was examining her with a serious expression while those dismal musings were flashing through her head faster than the speed of light. Then his face broke into a slow, sexy, teasing smile. It lengthened his eyes, made them do that crinkling thing at the corners.

She risked a glimpse into the silvery depths. 'I'm sorry I swiped you with that sonata.'

He nodded gravely. 'Okay. It's a long time since I was smacked by a beautiful woman. Exciting, though.' His voice was a velvet caress. 'Do you often…?'

'No.'

'Pity. You've got quite a good wrist action there. I'd have thought you'd had a bit of experience.' He saw her quick flush and, though his mouth grew grave, the smile still lurked in his eyes. Rueful, not unkind. Anything but unkind. 'Never mind. Apology accepted.'

Her heart quickened and she dragged her gaze away. She shouldn't have looked. She was, after all, Amber O'Neill, notorious push-over for charming heartbreakers. Next thing you knew she'd be starting to flirt, indulging in a little verbal sparring, giving him the husky laugh, luring him in, laying sultry glances on his mouth…

'Tsk, now look. You have dark smudges here…and here.' He lightly ran his thumb-tip under each eye. 'You'll have to cut out all this partying, Amber. You need to get some sleep.'

She ignored the soft imprint his thumb left on her skin, though lightning flickered through her skin cells and her sexual sensors went into a swoon. She hoped they didn't lose their giddy little heads.

She tried to distract him with conversation. If she didn't mention anything sexual, said nothing at all to do with his lips… Hers dried, and though she fought the urge she couldn't resist running her tongue-tip around them. She noticed how the wolf gleamed at once from his knowing eyes. Oh, Lord. He was reading her like a traffic light.

'What are you doing here, anyway?' She kept her tone polite. Not too interested, just neighbourly. 'Jean never mentioned you'd be staying.'

He nodded. 'It was pretty last-minute. A builder's knocking walls out of my house and it's currently unlivable. Jean's honeymoon has come at the right time.'

She frowned, thinking. 'I don't remember seeing you at the wedding.'

His face smoothed to become expressionless. 'I wasn't there.'

'Oh. What a shame you missed it. It was fantastic. What a party. Jean must be sorry you couldn't make it.'

He shrugged and gave a brief harsh laugh. 'She'd have been surprised if I had.'

His knee brushed hers and she momentarily closed her eyes. At least he sounded fond of Jean, she thought, savouring the sparks shooting up and down her leg. That was one thing about him. Another was his voice. It was so deep and dark, and in its way musical, as soothing to the ear as a lute.

She noticed with some surprise her headache had just about departed. That might have been down to the lute effect. Or even the knee factor. The truth was, sound was not her only sensitivity. Like the beguiling Eustacia Vye, she'd always had this intense vulnerability to certain masculine knees.

Face it, there were times she felt like a sensory theme park. Right now the lights were on, the music was playing and she was glowing from the inside out.

'It could be fantastic being here with you, Amber, or it could be…fantastic. What do you think?' His lean, smooth hands rippling the keys made the notes sound like velvet water. She could imagine those hands playing along her spine like that. Gentling her, caressing her. Stroking her languid limbs, her hair. Better than a dangling twig any day.

She gave a throaty laugh—not her day-to-day one. 'I wouldn't say you're *with* me, exactly.'

'Getting closer, though. Don't you think?' His arm curved around her and he patted her hip.

'You wish.' She shifted away a little—though not as far as all that. 'I don't think you've demonstrated your desirability as a neighbour yet, Guy.'

He responded with a low, sexy laugh that demonstrated confidence in his abilities, if nothing else. 'I'm working on it. Let's see. Can I tempt you to some wine?'

She rarely drank alcohol. Fruit and veggie juices were her preferred drinks. Wine was not the ballerina's friend. But, having assaulted him, she could hardly afford to be churlish. Besides, he smelled so deliciously male.

She lifted her shoulders. 'Wine would be—fine.'

He was gone a few minutes. After a short while she

heard him in Jean's kitchen, opening drawers and cupboards.

She drew some hard, deep breaths to fill her lungs. Her exhilarated blood felt all bubbly. She felt pleasantly high and in control, as she sometimes did on stage. It gave her the same sort of out-of-body freedom—as if she wasn't so much Amber as Amber's avatar.

Looking more devastating by the minute, Guy returned with two glasses of red, along with the bottle. Amber recognised the glasses as Jean's special wedding crystal. She accepted hers with a twinge of guilt. But, hey. She wasn't the police. And she wasn't in charge here, was she? Sometimes it was best to go with the flow.

They clinked glasses, Guy watching as she held her wine to her lips, his eyes shimmering with a warmth she knew only too well. Her blood quickened.

Desire was in the air.

'Tell me about yourself, Amber,' he said. 'What do you do besides worship the dead?'

'I'm a— I have the flower shop down in the arcade.'

He wrinkled his brow. 'Don't think I recall a florist's. Where is that? It must be tucked down an alleyway.'

'No, it's not.'

He set down his glass and started rippling the keys again.

She tried not to watch. The less chance she had to obsess on the lean hand finding a tune with such casual expertise the better. Or the other one. The one absently stroking so close to her breast.

'It's right at the end, near the street entrance. I—haven't had it long. There isn't much stock yet so it's not quite up and running. When I have more stock—more flowers, et cetera—you'll be likely to notice it then. I'll open up the street doors and put a lovely awning out in the street to catch the passing trade. Maybe in six months or so.' With loads of luck, time and dancing gigs.

He frowned and put his head on one side. 'Yeah? How does that work?'

She looked quickly at him. 'How do you mean?'

'Just that. When you start something *off* you need to start as you intend to…' He hesitated, his eyes calculating something she couldn't read, then all at once his gaze narrowed and he looked closely at her. 'Ah, now I can see why they called you Amber.' His voice deepened, as if he'd made a thrilling, almost arousing discovery. 'Look at that. They're not straight violet, after all. The irises have the most beautiful little amber flecks.'

Stirred, she felt herself flush, and gave an embarrassed laugh. 'Oh, honestly. Guys like you.'

Though he smiled, his eyes sharpened. 'What about guys like me?'

'You'd say anything. No one has violet eyes—except maybe Liz Taylor.'

'Hush. Where's the poetry in your soul? Anyway, that's only half true.' Absently, he took a lock of her hair, ran it through his fingers as if it were made of some rare, precious silk. Her hair follicles shivered with joy. 'There aren't any other guys like me. I'm the original one-off.'

Certainly better than a twig. With the wine warming her cockles, she was starting to feel quite languorous. Voluptuous, even. Gently she removed the tress from his fingers. 'They all say that.'

'Do they? I'm starting to wonder what sort of guys you know, Amber.' Then glancing at her, he gave a quick, rueful smile. 'Oh, sorry. I guess a woman like you… You'd be used to men wanting to impress you.' He flashed her a veiled look. 'Do you receive a lot of offers?'

She supposed there'd been a few. Though always from

people no one in their right mind would consider viable—
apart from Miguel. *Especially* Miguel.

Not caring to boast, she made a non-committal, so-so
sort of gesture. 'Oh, well…'

'I'm not surprised,' he said warmly. 'There are so many
of these blokes about. Operators looking for a beautiful
woman to hook up with.' He nodded, sighing. 'Yeah, I
know the type. First they use the old sweet talk routine to
soften you up. Then they manoeuvre you into a clinch.'
He glanced at her, his eyes gleaming. 'Or is that where
they start these days? With a kiss?'

As if he didn't know. Her heart bumped into double
time.

This conversation was heading in a certain direction,
but it was undeniably thrilling. It had been ages since
she'd felt on the verge of something truly dangerous and
fantastic. All right, so he was an operator of the worst
kind. She could be too, if she had to be. She hadn't taken
a celibacy vow yet, had she? Why else was she wearing
a push-up bra?

Right on cue Amber's avatar sashayed into centre stage
and met his gaze through Amber's lashes. 'I'm already
pretty soft, Guy,' she breathed through Amber's lips.
'There are times I prefer to go direct to the kiss.'

His eyes lit with a piercingly sensual gleam. He studied her, eyelids half lowered, reminding her even more of
that sleek, smiling wolf.

The summer evening tensed. A shivery excitement
prickled along her veins.

With his grey eyes shimmering, in dreamy slow motion
he raised a bronzed hand to push a loose strand of her hair
behind her ear. In the spot where his fingers connected her
skin sprang into tingling life. Softly he trailed one finger
over her cheek, down her throat to the hollow at its base.

Sensation rippled through her every nerve cell. Her lips parted as he stroked the delicate skin of her throat. Her skin fell into an enchantment. She saw his eyes drop to her mouth and darken and her heart gave a great bound.

She tilted her head, for a moment teetering on a magical edge of anticipation, then swiftly she leaned forward and pressed her lips to his. His sexy mouth felt, firm and so electrically alive, and tasted of wine. She moved her lips against his and a delicious fire sprang to life and danced along them.

His smooth hands slid up to cradle her head, and she leaned into him to gain a more comfortable position. He seized the initiative from her, intensifying the kiss to a searing, sensual charge. She felt something like a deep gasp whoosh through her, and her body shot into electric response as the tip of his tongue slid through to tangle with hers and tantalise the delicate tissues just inside her mouth.

Then, just when she thought desire was a pleasant hunger, his mouth took her tongue captive and sucked.

*Oh, baby.* Desire was no gentle longing. It was a raging furnace. She gave herself up to the mindless sensation. His beard rasping her skin, his vibrant chest firm and solid under her restless palms.

Liquid quivers shuddered through the top of her head, roused her through her breasts and thighs, down the backs of her knees to the tips of her curled up toes. His hands travelled caressingly up her arms, slid to her swelling breasts, while hers flexed on his biceps. Fire flamed in her blood, stirred all her secret, private places with yearning.

His breath mingled with hers and the masculine flavour of him went to her head like wine. He pulled her closer and she felt the friction of his hard chest pressing her nipples.

The blood boomed in her ears and lust swept her like a flame—wild, searing and erotic.

In the grip of the inferno, she thirsted to be closer. Struggling not to in any way diminish the connection, she kept glued to his lips while she squirmed her way onto his thighs. Straddling that impressive lap, she felt her appreciation of the kiss escalate to a whole new dimension.

As though divining her hunger, he tightened his arms around her and rocked her on the hard ridge of his erection with electrifying results. Pleasure roiled through her in waves.

And her body gasped for more. Much, much more. Until in one impassioned, over-enthusiastic plunge she rocked him right off the piano seat and onto the floor.

*Thwack.* She landed on top of him in a graceless tangle of arms and legs. Half groaning in a laughing complaint about her roughness, he adjusted his position beneath her. She laughed as well, while every inch of her was aware of the raw, virile flesh separated from hers by a couple of thin layers of material.

There was a moment when their laughter faded and they both stilled. His arms tightened around her again. She could feel his heart thumping against her chest while his masculine scent invaded her head. Or maybe that was her heart pounding in her ears like a jungle drum.

Anything could happen—but just like that? With a stranger? In Jean's flat?

She scrambled up, her head whirling. Adjusted her top. Smoothed her skirt. She might be a little drunk with that kiss, but parts of her brain were still connected.

Her host pulled himself up and adjusted his jeans. They almost managed to avoid one another's glances. The air sizzled with incompletion. It tugged at her breasts and feminine loins. Made her feel like doing something dangerous.

Guy felt every part of his body tingle to the imprint of

her soft, firm flesh. Was she about to slip through his fingers? Instinct told him not. Not if he played it easy.

He let his glance fall to where glimpses of her breasts tantalised at the edge of her shirt. Arousal had him in its grip. His erection was protesting the confinement of his underwear. Surely she must feel it too? Desire crackled in the air like electricity—a promise propelling them to an inevitable conclusion.

She *must* feel it.

Amber's gaze collided accidentally with his and she felt singed. She smoothed her hair. Maybe she should go home before his eyes carried her away. Home to her dark flat, with the sitting room furniture all jammed into the hall. The single lamp she read by. No company.

'I know what you're thinking.' he said softly. 'But you shouldn't go. Not yet.'

That piqued her pride. 'You don't know what I'm thinking.'

His eyes shimmered. 'Then show me. Let me in.'

As if she wasn't already intoxicated, she picked up her glass and drank more of the wicked, wicked wine. Glass in hand, she leaned on the piano and smiled. 'All right, tempter. Go on, then. Play for me.'

He frowned a little at first. She guessed he was disappointed. He'd had other entertainment in view. But he gave in with a gracious shrug and sat down at the piano.

He rested his hands loosely on the keys, then started into a song—some rare, long-forgotten tune that sidled into her heart with a haunting familiarity. He played it against the beat, like a true jazz man, drawing out its sexy sound.

Suddenly a door opened in her memory and a scene came rushing back.

Her mother and father, laughing and dancing in each

other's arms in the kitchen of their old house. When they were still together. When they still loved each other.

Now she knew the song. It was 'Ruby', an old number from a Ray Charles album her mother had loved. Lise had continued to play it long after Amber's father had left her. Left *them*.

It didn't even matter now that the lyrics weren't being sung. From down the decades Ray's beautiful dark golden voice was still in Amber's head, recorded there forever in high fidelity, the bittersweet pain of his song as fresh as ever.

Blame the wine or the song, but the music plucked unbearably at her heartstrings. Twisted her most vulnerable emotions and swamped her with nostalgia and regret.

Guy looked up and touched her with his gleaming glance. Something arced between them. Some mutual understanding.

Quickly she lowered her lashes, though she knew he'd seen her tears. But still he continued to play, wringing every last poignant drop from the song as if her response was only natural. Maybe it was then she confused the music with the man.

Fighting tears, she gazed at his lean, strong hands dancing on the keys, on her heart, and her desire bloomed into an intense hunger.

Devouring him with her eyes, she was shaken by a fierce wanton need to bite his mouth, lick his strong neck, feel his warm skin under her fingertips. All at once being near him was both anguish and ecstasy. Yearning for him while at the mercy of the song, she pressed her fingers hard to the piano. Caressed the silky wood, stroked the elegant lines, urgent in her longing to be touched and held.

Guy could hardly keep his eyes from her. Attuned to the quickening sexual current, he switched into one of his own songs. Sexed up the tempo in time with his accelerating desire.

At the change of melody Amber felt both sorry and relieved. At least without the song's weakening associations her defences managed to firm themselves up again. Good grief, she'd come close to an emotional meltdown. She was conscious of having allowed Guy, a *stranger*, to see too much, and everything in her scurried to cover up.

For goodness' sake, this was hardly the time or place for tears. This was the bewitching hour.

Slipping off her shoes, she crawled up onto the piano lid.

*Clunk.* The music hit a bump. Cool, casual Guy Wilder must be startled. Amber giggled with delight when she saw his stunned face. He was staring at her, his eyes gleaming with an amused and intensely sensual light.

He gave a deep sexy laugh. 'You bad, bad girl,' he said softly. 'What are you up to?'

Encouraged, she slithered across the lid to him, making herself as sinuous as a serpent. A voluptuous serpent, with a longing to feel the contact of hard, muscled man against her skin.

Her ravenous, tingling skin.

He stared at her, eyes ablaze, his hands suspended over the keys.

She rested her chin on her hands and smiled. 'Did you know I can do the splits?'

The piercing hot gleam in his eyes could have set her aflame. 'I'd really like to see that.'

The challenge in his husky voice revealed such a depth of wolfish excitement a laugh of pure exhilaration bubbled out of her. Amber O'Neill was flying high, as energised as if she'd just pirouetted right across the stage on points.

Loving her power to galvanise such warm admiration—

very warm, judging by the bulge in Guy's jeans—she ordered him to keep playing.

Guy was happy to accommodate. Eager, one might say. He did his best to comply, continuing to thump the keys while staring, mesmerised. At first she sat up, straight-backed, and tucked up her skirt into her pants' elastic.

Then, before his hypnotised gaze, she folded her supple self into the lotus position. Each time his fingers faltered on the keys she nodded at him to play on. He started into something—though who knew what? His hands were on an erratic auto-pilot, since every other part of him, from his fascinated gaze to his painful, throbbing erection, was riveted on her.

His brows lifted in disbelief as she smoothly stretched first her right leg, way out to ninety degrees at one side, then her left to the other. All the impossible way. Until both gorgeous legs made a perfect one-eighty. His gaze was riveted to the tender, crucial little bridge touching the piano lid in the middle. His jeans tightened unbearably.

She gazed down upon him like some oriental goddess, her eyes shadowed and mysterious. 'We call this the straddle position.'

Inside his constricting jeans, the skin of his engorged penis felt ready to burst.

Then, before his lustful gaze, she stretched her right arm over her head and with graceful ease laid her head down on her leg while she touched her left foot with her fingers, the long switch of her hair falling away from her neck.

Then she straightened her taut back and did the reverse, her left arm over her head, fingers touching her right foot. The graceful line of her body, the agonising beauty of her lithe form, her vulnerable neck, dragged at his heart.

It was too much for a guy two years on the sexual wagon.

He sprang up and seized her. With fire thundering in his blood, he lifted her off the piano and set her down on the floor.

Like a wild man, he took her sweet mouth in possession while somehow stripping off his clothes and fumbling with hers.

'Hurry, hurry,' she was trying to say through his frenzied kisses, as though he wasn't rushing as fast as any painfully aroused guy was humanly able.

When she stood naked before him, the beauty of her nude body made his insides tremble. Her breasts small and so achingly perfect. The areolae around the rosy, pouting nipples flushed with arousal. Her waist so slender his hands could have spanned it. The smooth curve of her hips and the pretty triangle of curls sent what was left of his sanity flying out of the window.

Free at last, his rampant erection reached the zenith of rock-hard demand. He stooped gingerly for his jeans and dug for the condom in his wallet, grateful to have one on hand.

For a moment she stood facing him, her eyes as hot as he knew his must be. Then she moved forward and put her arms around his neck, kissing his mouth and jaw, touching him, pressing herself to his chest and nuzzling his neck in the sort of confiding, feminine way that could weaken a man.

'You're beautiful,' she whispered, huskiness in her sweet voice. 'Such a strong, beautiful man.'

It tore at him in some way to reject her sweetness, but he couldn't encourage the softer expressions. Gently but firmly he put her away from him. He didn't require any further stimulation. And satisfaction could best be obtained for all concerned without too much of the demanding intimate stuff.

He pushed her onto the sofa. Deliciously willing, she lay there panting, scrutinising him, her lovely eyes dark and stormy with arousal. When he joined her, she met his passion with equal fervour.

He tried not to be rough or too greedy. While his lust raged over her fragile beauty with hands, lips and tongue, he drew on all his experience to please her. And she reciprocated, stroking and caressing him, playful and languid as a cat, while at the same time hungry. So primitively, devastatingly female.

When her moment was ripe, her sex as plump and juicy as a peach, he thrust his straining shaft into her gloriously tight aperture, unable to hold back a groan. It had been so long for him. The silky grip of her hot inner sheath felt like the closest he'd ever come to heaven.

Fearful of splitting her in two with his straining bulk, he took care with her at first, moving gently inside her to give her time to accustom to his size, watching the play of shadows on her face, feasting on her beauty.

Their eyes met. Locked. Something in her expression sent a rush of silly things to his tongue. Affectionate words, passionate phrases to express his appreciation, the sheer trembling pleasure in his heart. But some divine prudence held him back.

Best to avoid the lyrics.

Anyway, she arched her supple body under him then, locking her gorgeous legs around him to take him further in. He required no urging, and any random moment of tenderness that might have happened passed.

With the fiercest imaginable pleasure he plunged, thrusting his aching penis deep into her sweet, yielding flesh with rhythmic, ferocious vigour.

And she strove with him, tendons straining in her neck just as in his. In some ways—maybe it was her awesome gymnastic ability—he thought of her as his equal and his opposite. The supple muscles working under the skin of her slim abdomen thrilled and delighted him. Catapulted him towards his climax.

But he was still a gentleman where it counted.

With his urgent need for release straining at the very leash, he used all the control at his command to hold himself back. Concentrated on other things. Her sighs. The little cries issuing from deep in her throat. Her swollen mouth. And at last he was rewarded. Her orgasm blossomed. He saw it written in the flush of her skin, in the sort of ecstatic absorption that came over her face. Tears… were they tears?…spilled on her cheeks.

Then, blessedly, he felt her inside walls grip his grateful length with that bliss-making, rhythmic pull.

*Ohh.* Oh, Amber O'Neill.

With a groan he allowed himself to spill, surrendering to his own ecstasy.

It was cramped on Jean's sofa. After a few thundering heartbeats Guy hauled himself up and off her. Amber grimaced at the ridiculous blur in her eyes and gave them a hasty wipe with the back of her hand.

Smiling, she reached to touch Guy. Dragging his fingers through his hair, without any further eye contact he stumbled away in the direction of the bedrooms.

She heard taps go on and turned on her side, relaxed now that her heart had slowed its pounding, her skin feeling pleasant against the sofa fabric. She closed her eyes and snuggled into the cushions, grinning to herself.

How the world could change in a few short hours. Amber O'Neill had snagged herself a gorgeous playmate with no trouble whatsoever. A lovely, lovely man. Sexy. Musical. *Hot.* She really should knock on people's doors more often.

She waited so long she must have drifted into a little doze. After a while she woke to the chill on her cooling skin. There was no sign of Guy. She started to feel naked, and not in a good way.

She got up and started to dress, intending to go and investigate.

With her clothes on and the man missing, her amazing mood deflated. Taking stock of the scene, she hastened to plump up the sofa cushions, shuddering to imagine what Jean would have thought of her shenanigans.

Her shoes were under the piano. *Jean's* piano. How would she ever look Jean in the face again? She crawled under it to retrieve her shoes, and was slipping them on when Guy strolled in.

'Oh, Amber,' he said. 'Okay?' He smiled, but his glance slid off her before it could gain any foothold. He strolled to the coffee table and bent to switch on his laptop.

He was in fresh clothes, his hair gleaming wet. It looked as if he'd showered.

Questions flashed through her mind like quicksilver. Could he have been standing in the shower all that time? Why? Had he forgotten about her? It seemed as if he was avoiding looking at her.

She felt all at sea. Miguel had been cool, especially when he'd had something to hide, but this was *über*-cool.

She smiled, searching his face. 'Where'd you get to?'

He blinked rapidly. 'Well, I just…er…had something I needed to do. Look here, that was…that was really something, Amber. You're a beautiful woman. A very lovely woman. So, so sexy.' He took her arms and planted a little kiss on the corner of her mouth. 'Thing is,' he said, moving away, eyes screened by his lashes, 'I have an early start in the morning. Sorry if this seems a bit—abrupt, but I have things I need to prepare for work tomorrow.'

'Oh, right. Well…'

She looked searchingly at him, but he'd absented himself to somewhere remote. Shock must have fogged her brain, because she couldn't think up a sassy comment with which to ease the moment forward with a laugh and a wiggle.

She lifted her shoulders. 'Well, then. I'll be seeing you.' Stunned, confused and stinging, she walked to the door.

She opened it before he could, and was about to step outside when he murmured her name. She glanced back, her heart lifting.

But there was no farewell clinch. Just a brusque touch of her cheek. When he spoke his voice sounded gruff. 'Goodnight. Sleep well.'

She tried to get some words to form. Some cool words. But even Amber's avatar let her down this time and none would come.

She reached her front door, confusion and anger swelling in her chest.

She felt like such a fool. Such a silly, worthless fool.

# CHAPTER THREE

AMBER saw him in the arcade next morning, first thing, when she was hurrying home from her early dance class at the Wharf. Not many shops had yet opened their doors.

Guy appeared at the opposite end, loping up the near-deserted mall with a fluid, easy motion. He was in running shorts and a singlet, a sheen of perspiration on his neck and arms. The instant she spotted him her pulse revved up and her lungs forgot to breathe.

The gorgeous symmetry of all that muscle, bone and sinew working in symphony washed over her and left her feeling—raw. As any woman might feel after a long, anguished night curled up into a ball of shame and misery.

Thank goodness sheer exhaustion had mercifully blacked her out in the end.

She knew the exact moment he spotted her. There was a slight check in his gait, then he slowed to a walk. As he advanced towards her she tried to steady her face. She wasn't ready for this. She hadn't yet decided how to play it. How best to protect herself. If she had to share the lift with him she doubted she could trust herself to stay cool and unruffled for nine whole floors.

He drew level with her, his acute gaze taking in the shortish dress and the casual cardi she wore over her leotard, her sports carry-all.

'Er…hi.' He looked keenly at her with veiled eyes, then dropped his lashes. Perhaps she would detect something behind his casual greeting. Constraint. 'You're up early. Been to the gym?' He continued to gaze down at her, then turned with her towards the lift.

Amber pressed the button. 'Nope.'

'Yoga?'

'No.' She held her head high, not looking at him, but she could feel his quizzical gaze scrutinising her face. If he dared to make a joke about her flexibility…

The lift doors shuddered apart.

'Morning must make you brisk. I seem to recall you were much friendlier last night.' The mocking sensuality in his voice hit that raw spot in her vital organs, but she maintained her cool.

Stepping inside the narrow lift, she pressed for the ninth and turned deliberately to face him, arms extended to block his entrance. 'Must have been because you're such a warm guy, Guy.'

She smiled sweetly as the doors slid shut in his face.

With his coffee cooling, Guy clicked through his presentation to staff. Stared at it.

Hardly surprising, but he didn't take much in. What with last night constantly intruding, and now the encounter in the mall…

His fingers stilled on the mousepad. He hadn't been so aloof, had he? He'd tried to be gentle with her. Polite. He thought he'd expressed his sincere appreciation quite fulsomely.

He could admit to feeling a certain discomfort about the way things had gone down at the end of their sexy little interlude. Maybe she was right to some degree. He guessed he could have been smoother.

All right. *Kinder.* Thing was, he was out of practice.

The choking sensation rose in his chest and he squashed it down. He wasn't geared up for all the stuff with women.

Anyway, he rejected outright any blame for succumbing to sex. She'd been seductive, and so…so utterly…. For the whole of this morning's fifteen-kilometre run he'd been as preoccupied with recalling the highlights as a teenager after his first woman.

The *feel* of her. The sheer physical pleasure of holding her supple form in his arms. And at the same time her yielding softness. Her eyes, so gentle and giving and…

His heart quickened and he closed his eyelids. Even after the longest shower in history that softness had stayed on his skin the night through. Hell, what had come over him? He should have used more finesse.

But…

He couldn't risk getting into all that.

No doubt in this world, where men were the bad guys and women saints, his reserve at the end there could have come across as seeming casual. All right, cold.

Callous was far too harsh a term. Exploitative… Where had that sprung from?

*Never.*

He sprang up and paced. It was in no way true. If he wasn't the sucker he'd once been, he was still in every way a decent, caring and honourable guy. She couldn't deny she'd been equally enthusiastic. He hadn't promised her anything, had he?

This was just life. Amber O'Neill needed to toughen up. Sure, he'd noticed signs of emotion in her, but none of it had been down to *him*. He'd done nothing to bring that teary sparkle that had come and gone in her eyes. And for a woman to actually shed tears during sex…

What guy *would* cope?

He ignored the smart little voice piping, *The guy you used to be*. And he ignored the gnawing twinge that had been occupying his chest since he'd closed the door after her last night. Whatever had upset her was *not* his responsibility.

Men had to shield themselves or they could be swept along on a woman's emotions and end up a wreck before the eyes of the world.

He slammed the door on his old nightmare before it could properly materialise. Breathed carefully for a while. In. Out.

The wedding debacle had no more power to gut him. It was over now, the bad time long gone. He'd learned his lesson, and there'd be no more debacles for Guy Wilder.

If Amber O'Neill was too soft for the rough and tumble of casual sex she should look elsewhere for a playmate.

Regrettable, though, in some ways.

Amber chose one of her prettiest costumes: capri pants patterned in rose coloured daisies with a rose-pink top and heels. With a little make-up she looked cheery enough, and that was good. The customers didn't have to know she'd taken a few lacerations to the spirit.

Determined to swan through the day with a smile here and a sunbeam there, she made porridge—her favourite— then ended up washing it down the sink.

Food was impossible with her insides churning so fast. If only she hadn't encountered him in the mall.

There were so many things she could have said, but she was glad she'd restrained herself. Last night she might have felt like trash, but it was a sensation she'd experienced before. She just hadn't expected it. Not with him. He'd seemed so...lovely.

Anyway, no use brooding. Write him off as a mistake.

Wallowing in angst and recriminations wouldn't help. She'd found that out the hard way with Miguel, when her mother had needed her there every night. Some men were tone deaf to feelings.

Pity she could still make the same mistakes with that knowledge so deeply inscribed on her soul.

Anyway, forget Guy Wilder's smile and his crow's feet and his music. How charming he'd been until he'd achieved his… Oh. She flinched to think of it and her eyes were awash again.

She blotted them carefully with her fingers, but the tactic wasn't all that successful.

Great. Now she'd have to fix her mascara. What was wrong with her anyway? She was turning into an emotional wreck. She just mustn't *think* about it. It was too demoralising. It wasn't worth another second of her time.

She reminded herself of her resolutions. She wouldn't tolerate disrespect. Her next love, if she found one, would know how to value her. Gone were the days when she gave a man her all, while he took all he could.

She pressed her lips into a firm line. The old Amber was gone. The new Amber was sparing with her gifts. The *new* Amber took no prisoners.

Well, those were her resolves, at least, as she steeled herself to walk past Guy's door and into the lift.

Unlocking the shop door was a relief. At least here she had a safe haven from the perils of the ninth floor. And, since she was on her own for the day, she'd have no time to dwell on whether a man had deliberately conned her into believing he was a human being for the sake of an orgasm.

She'd barely received her daily flower delivery and commenced the task of sorting, before Roger, the smooth, bald CEO from Centre Management, strolled in.

He was doing the rounds, he said. Reminding everyone

of the next evening's residents' meeting. She noticed his shrewd, light eyes dart about, not missing a thing.

'Doesn't your lease come up for renewal soon?' he said blandly. 'Two months from tomorrow, isn't it?'

As if he didn't know. And as if she needed reminding.

He cast a measured glance at the shuttered glass wall. 'You know, Amber, some of our tenants consider this a very desirable location. That access to the street is valuable. Properly used, with a good display, the whole arcade would stand to benefit from that entrance being wide open and attractive.'

Amber was reminded of what one of her neighbours had recently said. Marc, the tenant of Homme, the menswear shop next door, had jokingly offered to swap premises with her. Homme could make a great splash at that entrance, Marc had enthused, making her and Serena laugh till they cried with his hilarious demonstrations of how he might arrange his favourite mannequins to attract attention.

Listening to Roger now, Amber wondered if Marc's suggestion had been more serious than she'd imagined.

After Roger drifted away, she sat disconsolately at the counter and stared around the shop. To make a worthwhile display out on the street as well as in the mall would require heaps more stock. Then there'd be the necessary awning, the stands, the cost of the sign...

Added to the cost of improving its interior, the shop's current takings weren't anywhere near sufficient to cover it.

She held her head in her hands. Even though she'd only had the shop a couple of months, she couldn't help feeling guilty. It was hers now, and like all the tenants there she had a responsibility in upholding the style of the arcade. With its wood panelling and leadlight framed windows, most of Kirribilli Mansions possessed an old-fashioned chic. *Most*.

Somehow her mother had always managed to wind the arcade management around her little finger. As far as Amber knew Fleur Elise had never been refurbished in the nine years since Lise had taken Ivy on. Amber often wondered if her mother would have had more success if she'd ignored Ivy's advice and taken another approach. Spent money to make money.

As so often these days, her thoughts crept to the possibility of a bank loan. Wasn't that how real business people commonly operated? Even without Roger's prompting, this felt like the moment to strike with the changes she wanted. And how else was she to do it?

Though what if Ivy was right? What if she purchased more stock and it all just withered and died? No return for the money, and no way to repay the loan?

What was it Guy had said about the need to begin as you intended to carry on?

She pushed thoughts of him away. Anyway, what would he—a songwriter—know about it? Sure, he seemed quite musical, but that was hardly a qualification for success in business.

At lunchtime she turned the 'Closed' sign to face outwards and strolled down to the deli for a sandwich. As she waited at the counter Marc, her mall neighbour, came up behind her with a cheery, 'Hi.'

He bent to look closely at her, his liquid dark eyes anxious. 'You're looking a bit peaky, darl. You haven't been listening to those poisonous rumours, have you?'

She lifted her brows. 'What rumours?'

'Oh, nothing to worry about. Just that silly old madam again. Take no notice of anything she says.'

Amber understood he was talking about Dianna

Delornay, the elegant proprietress of Madame, the shop across the mall from Fleur Elise.

'Come on, now. What did Di say?

He didn't take much coaxing. It seemed Di had requested a move to the other end of the mall. Apparently Di felt her glitzy little boutique was in danger of being embarrassed by the vibes from Fleur Elise.

'Goodness. *Embarrassed?*' Amber's amused little tinkling laugh was pure fraud to cover her indignation.

For heaven's sake. Surely Fleur Elise wasn't all that bad? She hadn't been aware of all this dissatisfaction with it when her mother was alive.

Despite Marc's sympathetic cooing, Amber walked back to her counter with doubt clouding her mind. Everyone knew Marc and Di were cronies. Maybe she should take up his offer of a swap.

Turning to examine the shutters that hadn't been opened for years, she tried to visualise the sort of display Marc would be likely to mount there. Underneath all his fooling, he seemed pretty much in love with his dreams of what he could do.

But what about *her* dreams? She couldn't suppress the thought that she'd given up her first big dream. She'd rushed home from Melbourne, left it all behind her, but for very good reasons. Her mother's need had been desperate. But would she truly give up on the shop's potential over a little bit of needed capital?

The trouble was she was *green*. Greener than one of her philodendrons. She was meant to be a dancer, not a businesswoman. With all the conflicting advice being flung at her from all directions she had no idea who to believe.

During the mid-afternoon lull she checked her Facebook page for news. Serena had posted her a funny comment.

Smiling, she typed a reply. Then, all by themselves, her fingers typed Guy's name into the search bar.

There were a few Guy Wilders in the world, but none of them appeared to be him. Probably a blessing. Who would want to know him better, anyway?

Her fingers, apparently. Because they went one further and Googled him.

Bingo.

She felt a small shock. There he was, looking impossibly crisp, clean-shaven and corporate. Involuntarily her blood started the same painful pounding she'd experienced this morning in the mall.

Breathing hard through her nostrils, she compressed her lips. He wasn't a genuine musician at all. He was in advertising. Wilder Solutions, his company was called. 'The most vibrant, up-and-coming ad co on the scene.' Right. She could imagine that.

She read through the whole site, stung by every glossy piece of spin. No doubt it was all true, and they were brilliant geniuses at selling things to people who didn't mind being cheated. Guy was certainly charming when he wanted to be. Persuasive. Seductive. He had all the gifts essential to a con man. She'd seen it with her own eyes. Felt the overwhelming effects. That was what professional liars were like.

He hadn't even bothered to tell her the truth about himself. What he *was*. In fact, he hadn't told her anything real about himself at all.

Guy stood outside Amber's door. He was in no way nervous. He was a guy, and he didn't have a nerve in his body. If something interpersonal needed fixing he'd do it, as he always did, with a few calm, succinct words.

Words were his forte. He shouldn't need to remind himself of that.

He braced himself, then knocked. No glow from inside illuminated the opaque glass of her fanlight, but although night had fallen he'd learned that didn't mean a thing. She could still be in there. In the dark. Doing who knew what.

He suddenly noticed his heart muscle thudding way too fast, and started as her low, musical voice issued through the door.

'Who is it?'

'It's me. Guy.' His words came out like a croak. What had gone wrong with his voice?

There was a long pause. As the silence stretched and stretched, Guy felt his tension tighten a couple of notches. Surely she wouldn't actually ignore him? Then a light went on and the door was snatched open.

'Well?'

He blinked. He couldn't see much of what she was wearing because she was only poking her head around the door. One thing, she seemed smaller all of a sudden. More petite. Vulnerable. Though the instant that emotive notion kindled in him he stamped it out before it could take hold.

He noticed behind her some sofa chairs and rolled-up rugs piled in the hall, while his ears picked up the gentle, plangent notes of some classical piece.

He squared his shoulders. 'Amber, could I—talk to you? I just wanted to—er…set something straight.'

Her brows arched. 'Oh, yes? What might that be?'

He pressed his lips together and scanned her unforgiving face. Whatever he'd done—*not* done—had offended deeply. 'Well, I don't really want to talk about it out here.'

She hesitated.

He read the wariness shadowing her eyes with a sudden rise in his blood pressure. For God's sake, did she think he was an axe murderer? 'I think it's a bit late to worry that I might try to steal your virtue.'

He may have sounded a bit terse, because she started to close the door. She'd have succeeded if hadn't moved swiftly to jam it open with his knee.

He should have remembered how startling the violet flash from her eyes could be. Miss Spitfire wasn't always all whipped cream and honey.

He held up his hands. 'All right. I'm sorry, I'm sorry. I shouldn't have said that. I only want to talk to you, I swear. Three minutes. Please?'

'I'm busy,' she said coolly. 'Write it down and slip it under the door.'

He was too stunned to resist her closing the door a second time. With a harsh, incredulous laugh, he shrugged and turned away.

Women. What did a man have to do?

# CHAPTER FOUR

AMBER woke early. At least something woke her.

She was barely out of her dream. A wicked, forbidden dream, in which her senses felt drenched in the taste, the scent, the sheer sexual heat of Guy Wilder.

Before she'd even managed to winch her eyes open her ears picked up the sound of a piano. Was she still in the dream? Vaguely she understood she was hearing a piece of Frederick Chopin's. Played very softly. One of the nocturnes.

*Oh.* Her insides smiled and curled over in bliss. Her favourite. Her most beautiful, all-time most romantic...

At some point she realised it was no dream.

As the poignant tones thrilled through her, playing havoc with her susceptible heartstrings, *manipulating* her, she lay unwillingly mesmerised, careful not to move, angrily straining for every last note.

With her ravished bones melting, she fought against herself.

Oh, come *on*. What was he up to?

Guy's steps slowed when the shop loomed into view. He needed to get it straight in his head what he wanted to say. Obviously last night had been a mistake. She'd probably assumed he'd rung her bell at that time intending to angle for more sex.

He felt the prickle of heat under his collar. A little from shame. *Admit it.* Although there was pride involved as well. He'd sincerely wanted to make amends. If that had involved kissing her...

For God's sake, he was a *man*. He couldn't deny that the desire to feel her in his arms again was torturing him. But he was a civilised person. He could admit when he was in the wrong.

Was this where he was at now? So inept at dealing with women they wouldn't give him the time of day? Anger and indecision pinched his gut. Surely that was a reason to cut his losses? Move on. Forget about her.

Despite his warring impulses, the nearer he approached the stronger his anticipation grew. Dammit it, he was curious to see her at work in her shop.

Like the others in the arcade, her window was framed in leadlight, though the pattern here was of flowers, with 'Fleur Elise' romantically inscribed at the top in flowing gold. No doubt the gold had gleamed brightly at one time. Now it looked faded, with curls of paint peeling from a couple edges.

A small array of blooms raised their heads in a brave little front display.

He had to look hard before he spotted Amber. She was inside among the flowerpots, standing with her back to him. Her blue floral dress was perfectly moulded to her pert little behind, and as she reached up for something on a shelf the movement pulled the hem high on her thighs.

High enough to reveal the long flowing muscles and slim shapely legs he remembered so well.

His blood quickened, but he controlled the response. He hadn't come here to be engulfed in another maelstrom of lust. Merely to apologise, if that was what it took. To recover some of his—whatever.

He could hardly believe he had to stop and consider his approach. A guy like him. With all his experience of women. In the past he'd have eased his way in with an irresistible line guaranteed to melt a glacier, if there'd been any of those left. These days he seemed to have lost the poetic touch.

Inside, Amber was just considering a redistribution of the shelves, with a view to somehow masking the tired paintwork, when a movement from the window caught the periphery of her eye.

*Aha.* A suit.

The man straightened up, and Amber's heart fishtailed like a trailer on an oil slick. Surely not. Not him. Not *here*.

She went hot and cold all over. With her heart racing like a fool's, she patted the coil of her hair and pinned the hydrangea more firmly behind her ear. After that Chopin this morning she couldn't say she was all that surprised he hadn't given up yet—but here of all places? Surely her workplace should be sacrosanct?

Why on earth had she told him where she worked?

She darted an anxious glance about. Oh, man. Chaos was threatening from every direction. For one thing Georgio, their supplier, hadn't turned up yet with the fresh blooms, so the display was even thinner than usual. For another Ivy could arrive at any minute. If she was here at the same time as Georgio her sharp, forensic eye would spot the extras Amber had sneaked into the stock order.

To make matters worse, Serena was coming in late. Which wouldn't be very comfortable, what with Ivy's antipathy towards her.

Taking his time to select a bouquet, Guy could feel his adrenaline pumping. He could tell she'd already spotted him by the way she was avoiding looking his way. Unless she slammed the shop doors in his face, this time she'd have to talk to him.

He checked. The doors were still open.

Positioning herself behind her counter, Amber composed her face. Cool. Not hostile. Indifferent. Unaffected. Though as he strolled in her muscles tensed. He was holding a bunch of pale pink and cream roses extended to avoid the drips. As he halted before her counter, his big masculine form somehow managed to control the entire space and soak up all the air.

She prayed her body didn't exhibit her awareness. Even after everything, seeing him looking so lean and sexy evoked that breathless, reckless feeling.

Today he was the straight, clean-shaven Guy from his other dimension. Her treacherous senses, apparently still steeped in the memory of passion, drooled at his crisp, freshly-washed scent. Sharply garbed in a charcoal suit, with pale blue shirt and darker blue silk tie, it was hard to reconcile him with the lazy, casual musician she'd thought he was. He looked sophisticated. Handsome.

His gaze captured hers. Their mutual intimacy blazed again in the air between them, as if his chiselled lips had only just that moment left hers tingling. Wanting.

He lowered his briefcase to the floor and handed over the flowers. He didn't smile, though his deep voice caressed her ear. 'Hi.'

With an effort of will she steeled herself to resist the force field. 'You don't have to do this.'

'Do what?'

'Come here. Buy flowers.'

'Why?' His sensuous lips made a wry curl. 'Were you intending to invite me for coffee?'

She felt the flame in her cheeks. 'There's no chance of that.'

'You're angry.'

Her heart thudded, but somehow she held her nerve. 'Not angry. Just—realistic.'

He hesitated. 'Look, Amber, I'm sorry if I—did anything to make you feel upset.'

She couldn't speak for a second. Then all the emotions she'd thought she had under control came bubbling to the surface like geysers.

'You need to know I am a human *being*, Guy.' Though her voice wobbled and her heart was whirring fit to burst, adrenaline lent her the necessary nerve to keep going. 'Not a—a *thing* a man can just *use*.' Her voice scraped at the last, but she fought back the ready tears with all her might.

Shock registered in his eyes, then a flush darkened his tan. 'Amber? *What?* I had no *intention*— That *wasn't* my…' His voice was hoarse. 'Believe me, I'm not that sort of guy. I—I really like you. I *respect* you. I'd never dream of treating you or—or any woman like…'

The glittering intensity in his storm cloud eyes might have been convincing if she hadn't been down here before. Seen a beautiful man's ability to lie like an angel.

She supplied his missing word for him. 'Trash.'

He flinched. Held very still. His lashes screened his gaze. She noticed his lean hands clench to fists, then saw him make the deliberate effort to relax them.

Though his shoulders retained their rigidity, he fired back, his gaze cool and level. 'That's quite a misinterpretation. I think you're reading too much into a small thing. Hell, it was never meant to be…' Shaking his head, he swung about, reefed his hand through his hair as if gathering more words. Then he turned back to her again. 'Look, as far as I'm concerned it was just a pleasant, casual eve-

ning between two consenting—people.' He added with a
small sardonic laugh, 'We're not exactly *engaged*.'

Curiously, her flush was outflanked by his. Before her
eyes he turned a dark, distressed red.

Clearly a champion at recovering his poise, though,
after he'd blinked once or twice his voice was as steady
as a rock. 'We need to sort this out rationally. Without all
this emotive language. Somewhere more…' He glanced
about as if his location was uncomfortable. 'Anyway, if
you could just listen.' He spread his hands. Hesitated.
'You're a gorgeous woman. But I'm not looking for any
sort of—ties. I guess the other night I may have thought…'

His flush was back in evidence. As no doubt was hers,
though indignation was her excuse.

'What? That I was a slut? Easily disposable?'

He waved his hands in shocked denial and was protesting in some non-emotive, rational language when Georgio
poked his head in the door.

'Helloo—helloo.'

Amber started, dragged from the conversation. There
was Georgio, grinning and as bright and breezy as if his
delivery was right on time.

'Oh.' Torn between conflicting urgencies, she gave Guy
a cold look, then turned away. Why did even framing
those words herself have to hurt her so much? Grabbing
her apron, she slipped it over her head and dashed outside
to the street, where Georgio had parked his van.

Guy hung there in limbo, his brain still reeling from
the damning things she'd said. Oh, he got it all right. In
shock and utter shame he understood that as far as Amber
O'Neill was concerned he was a barbarian. The lowest
of the low. While full and total comprehension seeped
through his brain and into his gut like a toxin, he tried to
stem the flow with some upbeat self-protective guy talk.

Since when did sex have to be so complicated? He hadn't signed any contract. He didn't *do* all this stuff any more.

His *heart*, if that was what people wanted to call that particular bunch of chemicals, had been cauterised for all time. And rightly so. The sucker had caused him enough grief. For goodness' sake, near enough despair.

From outside, Amber's light and lovely voice floated back to him. 'Georgio, I've been trying to call you for ages. What…?'

A minute later she reappeared, assisting an old guy to manoeuvre a trolley-load of boxes into a room at the rear. The old guy was puffing and rattling on about a hold-up in the tunnel.

While Guy continued to grapple with his devastated ego a short woman with an uncompromising brown fringe walked in and, without any greeting, straight past him through to the back room where the stock was being unloaded.

Her sharp voice penetrated to the front of the shop. 'What's this, Amber? Are they just getting here now? What the hell do you think this is, Georgio? Do you know what time it is? And, here. We don't want these. Or these. Take them back.'

Guy pricked up his ears. For a second he ignored his blistered pride and eavesdropped on the conversation in the back room.

'Wait, Georgio. No, don't take them back.' It was Amber's voice. 'I ordered them, Ivy. I want them.'

There was a rapid murmured exchange, finishing with, 'I thought I'd explained this yesterday, Amber. Here— give me that invoice. Where's Serena, anyway? *She* should have sorted this lot.'

'Serena's had a problem with her…'

Guy saw a harassed-looking Amber pass by the open doorway. She halted when she caught sight of him still standing there.

'Oh.' She came flying across the room, flushed, hair dishevelled, wiping her hands on her apron. 'Look,' she said urgently, 'I can't talk now. Our delivery's arrived late and everything's in a bit of a shemozzle.' Catching sight of the roses, she said impatiently, 'Do you really want these?'

Unwilling to be ejected so summarily after he'd been downgraded to the level of brute, with no right of appeal, he insisted. 'Sure I do. Of course.'

Flustered, perhaps distracted by the voices issuing from the back room, she wrapped them in silver paper, tied a ribbon around them, then sped through the transaction. It was clear to Guy by the way her fingers flew over the keys that she was eager to be rid of him ASAP.

She thrust his card and the receipt towards him. He accepted them, then snaked his hand out to grab hers. 'Meet me in the city after work.'

Her hand quivered in his, cool and burning hot at the same time, but she yanked it away fast. There was a momentary spark in her violet eyes that he could almost have sworn teetered on capitulation, then they chilled pretty convincingly.

'No. There's no point.'

Hope died hard. He might have deserved punishment, but the rejection hit the old nerve. A man should have at least *half* a right to defend himself before execution.

He was about to intensify his attempt to retrieve some of his honour when the small woman reappeared from the back room, muttering, 'That Serena's useless.'

Amber turned her gaze to the woman. 'She really couldn't help it, Ivy,' she said quietly. 'Her babysitter was sick. She rang in to warn me.'

'You're too soft, Amber,' the woman snapped. 'You'd swallow anything. Yes?' This to Guy. 'You still here? Can we help you?'

Guy saw the quick flush flare in Amber's cheeks.

'It's all right, Ivy. I'm helping the customer.'

'He's had time to help himself to the whole shop by now.'

*'Ivy.'*

The small woman threw up her hands and stomped into the back room, where her sharp voice could be heard harrying the old man.

Conscious of more tension in the room than just his own, Guy picked up his briefcase and the roses. Refusing to accept defeat, he gazed down at Amber. 'We'll finish this later. Do you know the Shangri-la Hotel?'

Her eyes darkened, her lashes fluttering down to hide them. She shook her head. 'No. Look, I have to attend a meeting tonight at six. Anyway, I told you. There's no point.' She hardened her expression. 'No *point.*'

He felt his gut tighten. There was a point for him. He couldn't leave it like this. Not like this.

Luckily, when the chips were down, inspiration could strike him. Right at that moment he had an image of his aunt's face, and along with it the calendar she kept pinned to her fridge with all her social commitments.

Something about a meeting of the Kirribilli Mansions Residents' Committee. At six p.m. on the thirtieth. Wasn't this the thirtieth?

# CHAPTER FIVE

AT THE end of a difficult day, Amber wished, rather than pressing for the lift to take her to the residents' meeting, she could be far away. On a Pacific cruise, like Jean, or better still the planet Saturn.

Somewhere free from the threat of hungry wolves with sexy mouths. The sooner the honeymooners were home, the happier she would be. The safer. The sheer energy cost of having met Guy Wilder was exhausting. *Twice* while he'd been in the shop this morning she'd been tempted to soften. Twice. She'd actually, for a fleeting instant, considered his demand to meet him. Visions of exotic temptations at the Shangri-la had floated in her imagination for a teensy, tantalising second. Before her brain had cut in.

Give in to that and where would her self respect be?

After he'd gone, though, she hadn't been able to stop thinking of his expression when he'd turned to leave. The lines of his face had tautened to make him look so—grim.

*Oh, Amber. Please.* What was wrong with her? Had she forgotten everything she'd learned? She stiffened her spine and shoulders in resistance for a second or so, then let them slump.

Who was she kidding? She knew what was amiss, all right. Having once tasted the wine, the Eustacia Vye in her was craving another sip. A stroll under the gum trees.

Perhaps even a swipe of her head from the palm fronds
at the Shangri-la.

She had to fight it—*had* to. Hadn't she learned only
too well how powerfully that addiction could take hold?
It was so insidious. The effects of even that single sexual
encounter had sunk so deep. Everything about him seemed
to have crept into her senses. His hands, his eyebrows.
That way he had of considering her every light word as if
it had been carved in concrete.

And it was becoming blindingly clear that, regardless
of the things she *said* to him, every moment she spent in
his dangerous company only fuelled the flames.

To add to her quandary, this afternoon she'd received
an e-card in her junk mail from Jean.

Having a sensational time!!! Everything fantastic.
The food, the wine, the ports, the people. Look out
for Guy, won't you? Mind you give him some TLC.
Lots of love x

Amber had puzzled over it for minutes. TLC for *Guy*?
Was Jean kidding? Did she realise what TLC meant?
Maybe she had her acronyms mixed up.

The residents' meetings were usually lacklustre affairs,
though the oldies got a kick from the gossip. Amber had
been to a few of the smaller ones, but tonight's was the
big annual affair, where the residents and arcade tenants
combined.

Though everyone she'd talked to in the mall seemed to
be planning to attend, Amber felt tempted to bypass the
entire event. Go straight home and soak in a long, soothing, chamomile-scented bath. Wash her hair and paint her
toenails. Chill and stop thinking of wine and—that man.

If only tonight's gathering hadn't been slated as espe-

cially important. Roger had told her that once the tower
residents' issues were dealt with the business owners
would be discussing future directions in the arcade.

A worrying thought occurred to her. What if they dis-
cussed her shop and she wasn't there to defend herself?
Though surely they wouldn't do anything so unprofes-
sional? The shopkeepers were all friends, in a low-key sort
of way. Regardless of Roger's quiet hints to her, everyone
was always treated with consideration at the meetings.

With a sigh, she braced herself to be bored, pasted on
a smile, and walked into the assembly room.

*What?* She nearly choked. Shock speared through her
from head to toe.

Guy was there.

Not only was he there, he was occupying Jean's place
at the official desk. But why? As secretary of the committee, it was Jean's usual role to take the minutes. In her
absence anyone else could do it. But there *he* was, laptop
open before him, conversing with people, as relaxed and
confident as if he belonged there.

On the other side of the room, some instinct or vibration
on the air made Guy glance up. Despite what had happened
between them this morning, his heart-rate bumped up a
notch. Spring had walked into the room. She was hesitating just inside the rear entrance, as slender and fragile in
her flowery dress as an iris.

He noticed her stiffen and the set of her delicate jaw
firm slightly.

She'd spotted him, then. As a spontaneous response,
it was hardly flattering. More like a skewer through the
guts. One way or another, he really needed to fix things
with her.

Amber's heart thumped with the stress. What was

he doing here? Invading her professional life? This was wrong. All wrong.

An elderly major from the eighth floor was bending his ear while Guy lounged in his chair nodding, occasionally smiling. She could see him charming the old digger's socks off. Smiling. Convincing the old boy there was nothing in the world as interesting as his reminiscences about the war.

Guy looked around at her then and their eyes clashed. She saw his face stiffen for an instant, but that might have only been a shadow because it was gone in a trice. He just nodded coolly and went back to the war story as if she was no one of importance.

Strangely, though, in spite of her cynicism, she had the strongest sensation his cool was a total sham. He was as aware of her as if there was no one else in the room.

She knew it with absolute certainty. Because although the room was filling up, buzzing with people, groups chatting here and there, the usual throng gossiping by the desk, she felt gripped by exactly the same obsessive awareness herself.

Heaven forgive her, but right at this moment no one else in the room existed. In fact, it wouldn't have come as a surprise to her to learn that he'd engineered his way into the meeting specifically to pursue her. But why?

Her tension increased. Had he thought she was playing some game with him this morning? Didn't he understand she wanted nothing of him?

She waited until a couple of people blocked his line of sight before sidling up to the table and reaching through a chink between bodies for a copy of the agenda.

Before she could snatch one Guy's hand was there first. His fingertips brushed hers, and it was like a couple of electric wires crossing. As his intense darkened eyes clashed with hers the breath was knocked from her lungs.

She had a wild fleeting impression of showering sparks, sizzling air, walls shaking.

He handed her the sheet. 'Hello, Amber.' His voice had that darker, quarry pit quality from the other night.

'Oh. Hi…er…thanks.'

She backed away, then scouted about for a chair, choosing an inconspicuous place near the exit, from where she could keep her eye on the desk without seeming to.

She wasn't shaking, was she? No. She just felt…a little…shaken up.

She felt pretty sure the thudding going on in her chest was from adrenaline. But if he was hoping to succeed in seducing her again by intruding into every area of her life he was wasting his time. Nothing he said could make the way he'd treated her acceptable. *Nothing*.

That was exactly the trap she'd fallen into with Miguel. Time and time again. He'd make her feel sorry for him, she'd forgive him, then he'd act like an even bigger jerk than before.

Across the room she caught sight of Roger in a huddle with some of her arcade neighbours, including Marc and Di Delornay.

Amber glanced again. Was there was something strange about them? They looked quite secretive. Conspiratorial, almost. Were they plotting something?

Di looked over at that moment and crossed gazes with her, then muttered something out of the side of her mouth. Worryingly, the others all stopped talking. Some cast Amber covert glances, then the group broke up.

Had they been talking about *her*? What about? Something to do with the shop?

She tightened her hold on the agenda. Too bad. They could talk all they liked. She had nothing to apologise for, and right now more pressing issues to deal with. Despite her edgy pulse, she threw them all a breezy wave and pretended to read.

If he had to be here, it was a good thing Guy was taking the minutes, actually. Because it meant she could slip away before the meeting ended. Before he had a chance to waylay her. He'd be stuck here, noting down every last word.

The moment arrived when the hum of conversation eased. The chairperson, large in cyclamen, gathered her majestic bulk and called the meeting to order.

'Most of you will have met Jean's nephew, Guy,' the chair announced, twiddling her pearls and beaming through the diamanté frames of her specs. 'Guy's kindly offered to fill in for Jean in her absence. I think you'll agree it's wonderful of this busy, busy man to give us a slice of his precious time.'

'Hear, hear.'

There was a small round of applause, then the meeting got underway, with sundry minor items being thoroughly dissected by the residents while the business owners sighed and stared at the ceiling. Guy seemed to take his secretarial role seriously, typing occasional bursts on his keyboard and listening intently.

Every so often the chair turned to him and asked for his opinion, just as she usually did with Jean, and he answered with such calm, intelligent reason Amber gritted her teeth. All right, she could admit he appeared to have a certain authority.

She could see people warming to him. And why wouldn't they? He was charming. *She'd* warmed to him. And he had that sophisticated aura of the city hanging about him. Honestly, every time she saw him he looked less and less like the musician she'd made love with. Though how her mind could even *think* those words in reference to him without *choking*…

No, now he looked quite the slick, corporate advertising man he appeared on his website. A purely objective scan of his face revealed his five o'clock shadow, advanced since this morning. And it so suited his lean face. Drew aching attention to the sensuousness of his chiselled mouth. A mouth she'd kissed.

Had kissed her.

That trick he had of smiling with his eyes as he listened to someone…

Involuntarily, her insides curled over. She fixed her gaze firmly on her agenda. Looking at him was painful.

If everyone here knew how deeply cold and ruthless he was in his private life, they wouldn't all be queuing up to agree with his opinion. As if he was now the final authority on how to deal with everything from the City Council to the janitor. Considering his casual way of treating Jean's flat, there was such irony in that.

Amber's eye fell on the last item on the agenda. 'Tenancy Relocations'. What was that about? Marc was probably hoping it referred to Fleur Elise.

Guy gave half his brain to the proceedings, sifting out the crucial points with the expertise of experience. The other half was focused on framing some words. Lyrics had never been so tricky. How had he ever made such a complete hash as he had this morning?

Still, was there a woman in the world who was straightforward? This morning he'd finally comprehended something about Amber. It had rocked him. Made his heart clench at odd moments all day. It was no wonder his conscience was burning like hell.

He'd seen it in her before without understanding. But now…

He hated this feeling of having bruised something delicate. It had hit him with blinding force that Amber O'Neill was as tender as one of her own rose petals.

Roger, the CEO, rose from his chair, still blathering, and walked around to plant himself before the assembly.

Foiled by good manners from making an early escape, Amber shifted restlessly in her chair. How much longer did she have to stay here, avoiding Guy Wilder's piercing gaze?

Roger cleared his throat and she gave him her unwilling attention.

'As you know, in a centre like this it's the management's job to guarantee that every business maintains a professional standard. I've been in discussion with some of you about your particular issues, and most tenants—' here he cast an approving look around the room '—in fact I think I can report that nearly *all* have either complied already or have signed the agreement to meet our renovation deadline.' He frowned down at his notes, then scanned the assembled faces. 'There are still a couple of people who haven't settled their plans with us yet.'

Amber's insides lurched as his probing gaze scanned the faces, then settled on her.

'Just wondering how you're travelling with this, Amber? I have at least one applicant willing to lease your location if you don't want to keep it on. Let's see—your lease expires two months from now. Have you made any arrangements to move out of the arcade?'

Amber blenched with shock. To *move*?

Her brain seemed to slow down to a sort of paralysis. Was he being serious? Could he really be saying what it sounded like?

Hot with confusion, she grew aware of all eyes turning in her direction. With a pang she realised Guy was witnessing this. Her public humiliation.

With all her being she wished he was a hundred miles away.

Unable to help herself, she shot a covert glance in his direction. Not focusing directly, of course, but she could feel his gaze torching her face. She felt herself turning a slow, agonised red.

If there truly was a heavenly host, now was the time for them to sink her through the carpet. She could sense everyone waiting. What did they expect her to say? They knew she didn't want to move. She couldn't afford to. Roger knew it. They all knew it.

Guy sat very still, a pulse ticking in his temples, uncomfortably conscious of her embarrassment. He willed her to speak.

At last.

Her voice when it came was low and sweet. Proud. Scared.

'I wasn't planning any such thing. My mother bought this lease and I'm hoping to extend it. I'm intending to stay right here.'

'Ah.' Roger smiled again smoothly. 'Well, good…good.' He flicked a glance towards one of the groups. 'Then, in that case, I have some copies of the agreement here with me now, Amber. For everyone's peace of mind I think it best we settle this for good and all. Right here, right now. Everyone okay with that?'

Guy noted the chorus of mixed responses. It seemed not everyone thought the matter should be handled in a public forum. Thank God there were a few good people who murmured dissent. He studied the guy handling the discussion. What was going on here, really? Why publicly embarrass one of his tenants? There had to be a hidden agenda.

Conscious of feeling under attack, Amber noticed to

her eternal gratitude that some people sprang to her defence. Even the fruiterer spoke up.

'Mate, give the girl a break. She's only had the reins a few weeks. Let her find her feet. We can all wait a little longer.'

Though not all her friends acted like friends.

'No, people. *No.* That is *so* not the point.' Marc sprang to his feet and clutched his sideburns in agitation, his huge dark eyes showing their whites. 'This is the moment to strike. We all need certainty that this issue is being dealt with. I for one need *closure.*'

In shock, Amber gasped, *'What?* Closure of my shop?'

'I'm afraid I agree with some of what Marc says,' Roger said. 'With all due respect to your recent situation, Amber, people here have a legitimate right to expect certainty. Are you prepared to meet your obligations to us all and have your premises renovated within two months?'

Amber stared at him. She tried to swallow, but her saliva evaporated. It was mortifying, hearing the pleading note in her own voice. 'Oh. Does it *have* to be within two months?'

'I'm afraid it does. With respect, we tried for several years to negotiate with your mother to do the same thing. I'm afraid our patience has run out. Other owners are expressing their concern about the lack of an appealing entrance at that end of the mall.'

Guy almost felt the flinch in Amber's face as a small vociferous group swarmed with offers to take over her location.

'It's so dreary down there I'm ashamed to be seen coming in that way,' one woman declared.

'Oh, I know,' one heavily made-up harpy drawled, with posh, plummy vowels. 'If *I* had the location Madame would have a stunning, very chic display. I'd want it to be *vibrant*.' She flung out her bejewelled hands. 'Eye-catching enough to attract the traffic trade and pull customers in from the street.'

The approving smirk the manager turned on the woman opened Guy's eyes as to what might be going on.

He flicked a glance at Amber. Sure, none of this had anything to do with him. He was here purely to smooth things over with her, not to get involved in the politics of the place. Still, the eye messages he caught passing between some of the stakeholders made him realise he was witnessing an ambush.

Did these jackals have any idea of the damage they were doing?

The old Guy must still be in him somewhere, because he burned to spring up, stride across the room and punch the disgraceful manager in the face for encouraging this free-for-all. If he could have knocked a few of the scavengers flat on their faces at the same time he'd have relished it.

Then he wanted to grab Amber O'Neill and remove her from the brutality.

Take her somewhere quiet and green, by a flowing stream. Soothe her, stroke her beautiful proud face and neck. Hold her to him. Ease her down on the soft grass.

Kiss her.

Rock her in his arms.

Amber heard the insults flying thick and fast in horrified disbelief. Surely she was in a nightmare? People she'd thought were her mother's friends were scrabbling now for her location before she was cold in her grave.

'Of course it's up to you who you decide to give it to, Rog.' That was Di Delornay, beaming at Roger. 'It's pretty clear Amber isn't capable of doing it justice.'

Incensed, Amber sat upright, straightened her shoulders. 'Now, wait just a minute there, Di. While I hold the lease it's up to me. I *can* do justice to it. I fully intend to open Fleur Elise's doors to the street.'

Marc rolled his eyes. 'We'll believe that when we see it, sweetikins.'

The heat rose in Amber's cheeks, along with her blood pressure. 'You *will* see it. You would have before, except… Well, Mum always intended to do that too, but Ivy said… And Mum… Well, she had difficulties…' Her throat thickened and her voice wobbled. 'It wasn't—easy for her, with everything she had to… And then when she got sick…' Predictably, her eyes swam, and she had and stop to struggle for control.

There was an embarrassed pause, then people started shuffling and coughing. Some of the same people who'd been standing beside her at her mother's graveside only eleven short weeks before. Some of them had been weeping too. Some of them had had their arms around her, while others had patted Ivy and tried to soothe her hoarse, inconsolable sobs.

Roger cleared his throat. 'I'm sure we all sympathise, Amber, but I have to be fair to *all* tenants. Before we can approve an extension to your lease I need to know what you have in place to improve your shop's performance. If anything,' he added grimly.

'Well…' Blinking fast, she twisted her hands in her lap.

There was an excruciating pause. People were avoiding meeting her eyes.

Guy held his breath. He saw the red tide of shame rise to Amber's hairline. With a sharp twist in his chest he recognised exactly how Amber O'Neill felt at this moment. Her brave, straight back, her dignified, distressed face transported him with painful immediacy right back to a moment in time he'd never wanted to revisit.

With grim finality he closed his keyboard and opened his briefcase, the clicks of the catches loud in the expectant silence.

Terrified her tenancy was slipping away from her, Amber knew she had to say something. *Anything.* She drew a shaky breath.

'I intend to expand the range of our stock and to make a stronger impression. I've only been here a few weeks, and I just need time. To paint it and everything. I know it needs brightening up, and you all have a right to feel… But—I *am*—I'm doing everything I can to—to…'

The honest truth was she had a million ideas a day. But right at this moment, when she had to produce them under intense pressure from a gang, in a life-or-death situation with the heat on, her brain completely dried up. As did her words.

'I—I really am doing *everything*…'

Her tortured croak hung on the air, substanceless, unconvincing. Her bread and butter, her commitment to Serena and Ivy, teetered on the edge of a cliff.

Then from out of the haze Guy Wilder's deep voice cut through the strained vibrations with sure, casual clarity. 'Don't forget the advertising campaign we've planned, Amber. That kicks off after you've done the interior. And you're starting that next week. Isn't that what you told me you'd decided?'

She stared at him, dumbfounded. Heads swivelled around to him in surprise. With measured calm he got up from his desk and strolled around to join Roger, his tall, lean frame stealing Roger's space.

He held out his hand with cool authority. 'Did you say you have a copy of that agreement, Roger? Mind if I take a look?'

'It's all absolutely above-board,' Roger said huffily as

Guy neatly whipped it from Roger's open folder and perused it. 'If you have any legal training—as *I* have—you'll see it's a standard agreement used by all mall managements. Everyone else has seen fit to sign. I'm prepared to witness Amber's signature now, if she really *is* taking steps...'

The owners broke into a murmured hubbub while Guy took his time, examining the document thoroughly with a meditative frown.

After a minute or so he gave an easy shrug and strolled with the document to where Amber sat hypnotised on her chair. 'Might as well, Amber,' he said. 'Now's as good a time as any. Have you read this? All this stuff is totally in line with your plan.'

She looked hard at him, fascinated. 'Is it? My...?'

He smiled. 'Your plan to hire *me*. Of course.'

# CHAPTER SIX

THE Kirribilli Mansions lifts were far too cramped. Especially when shared with six feet or so of unscrupulous, scheming man.

Guy Wilder leaned against one wall, nonchalant, hands shoved in pockets, while Amber leaned against the opposing one. Contradictions wrestled for supremacy in her bamboozled brain. He didn't want any ties, yet he seemed to be pursuing her. *Seemed* to be. Even after she'd rejected him. She'd never forgive him—*couldn't* if she had any pride—but he'd rescued her from a nightmare.

Was it some ploy? Some devious opportunistic trick to get her back on Jean's sofa?

Arousing though that image might be, she must not allow herself to forget. Essentially he was a cold, cold man.

Though hot.

Smoking hot.

The lean solidity of his hard-muscled person was hard to ignore. Up this close, and seemingly accessible, naturally he exerted a strong magnetic pull.

A treacherous flame licked through her insides and warmed her intimate parts. Well, she was only human. With his pleasantly clean, masculine scent taunting her senses, the crispness of his hair and eyebrows making her fingertips itch, Ms E. Vye was hovering over her shoulder.

She met his grey gaze. 'Why did you do it?'

His brows lifted. 'Do what?'

'Make up that story? About me hiring you?'

He gave a lazy shrug. 'I didn't like that Roger's face. People who smirk always worry me.'

The lift stopped at the ninth floor and the doors cranked open. It took a second for their arrival to register with her, so caught up was she in the moment.

Once she'd extracted herself from the confined space, she turned to him in the hall. 'No, really. Why did you?'

He flickered a considering glance over her, then dropped his eyes. 'Maybe I don't like to see someone being bullied by a gang.'

Her heart clenched in acknowledgement. There was truth to his words. That was exactly how she had perceived the event herself. Violent. Uncivilised. People she'd liked and trusted leaping onto the bandwagon to attack. But could she bear sympathy from him?

'But it wasn't everyone,' she said quickly. 'Only a few.'

'An influential few.'

She flushed as though the shame was hers, and Guy was reminded of how he'd felt after his public evisceration. There was nothing more humiliating than that look of pity in a would-be comforter's eyes. Pity could feel so dangerously close to contempt.

'Maybe.' Amber lifted a shoulder. 'I certainly wasn't expecting any of that. But I hope you weren't thinking I was some kind of victim?'

'Hell, no.'

Each of their apartment doors was close at hand. She hunted around in her bag for her keys, her skin prickling with awareness of him. At least the ice had been broken. She supposed they could be on normal speaking terms now.

Normal for neighbours, that was. Not for sleeping partners. Though sleeping, *per se,* had never happened between them. Only sex. And the sex could certainly never be repeated. Even if he had saved her life from a horde of butchers waving knives. Not unless he came up with a corker of a satisfactory explanation for his poor performance in the afterglow department.

In fact it would be best not to think about him in that way at all. Forget the sex and how it had felt skin to skin with him. Chest to chest. Eliminate all that. All thoughts of kissing.

She paused to level a firm glance at him. 'We O'Neills can defend ourselves.'

'Oh, I know that.' He made a wry face. 'Actually, I was impressed by the way you stood up to them. Reminded me of a warrior princess.'

'Oh, right.' She rolled her eyes. Might even have laughed except that right then, despite her warrior tendencies, she seemed to be seized with a fit of the shudders.

'Are you all right?' He moved a little closer to her.

He looked serious, concerned, even, as if he thought she might be about to keel over. His hands twitched towards her, then changed their minds and curled into fists.

'Of course.' She rubbed her arms to warm them, and his frown deepened.

'You're probably in shock. You should have a hot drink.'

'Shock? *No.* I'm fine. Just a bit empty. Haven't eaten much today.' Oh, God, why tell him that? Why not just tell him outright that since he'd inflicted the wound on her soul she couldn't eat, think or concentrate properly on anything but him? And on passion, pain, and what it meant about her that she was attracted to people like him? 'I'm just getting over how vicious some people were.'

'Mmm.' He was still looking her over with concern.

Well, it looked like concern. Unless she was reading too much into things again. 'Greedy is the word that springs to mind.'

Again, his words struck a chord. That was exactly how she'd viewed it herself. 'Really? Did you think so?'

'Of course,' he said warmly. 'They were just trying to get their grubby hands on your location. How long since you've had the shop?'

'Ten weeks.'

He curled his lip in disgust. 'So they decided this was their chance? Before you had time to settle in?'

'Seems that way. Though they probably thought they had right on their side. The shop could certainly do with a make-over. Somehow I'll have to organise that now.' She heaved a worried sigh. Now all she had to do was find a way to fulfil the contract she'd signed.

'Can I have those?'

She was too surprised to react. He just casually slipped the keys from her grasp and unlocked her door.

'Do you have any tea in here?' He was already half inside, holding the door wide.

'I do. But, look, don't *you* worry. I'll be…'

He didn't appear to hear her protest. He urged her in, clearly intending to come along. Her trouble was her mother had instilled manners into her. Even if a rattlesnake had insisted on hustling her into her flat five minutes after it had seen off her enemies, she would probably have complied gracefully.

While in *his* case…

Well, it was impossible to be deliberately rude to a man who'd just saved her bacon—even him. Before she knew it she was politely pointing out the easiest route around and over the furniture in the hall. Lucky he couldn't see her face. Her mouth and jaw were locked into a grimace of discomfort.

She absolutely *prickled* with the strange and disturbing sensation of seeing Guy Wilder opening her cupboard doors, wresting the kettle from her nerveless grip and taking charge of her kitchen.

Her very small kitchen. Smaller than it had ever been before.

She sat tensely at the table. While boiling water was poured, milk and sugar located, strange and disturbing notions of what he might be up to assailed her brain.

On the surface he was all cool efficiency. He gave no clue as to whether he was intending to throw her onto the nearest sofa or not. Just as well, because hers was in the hall, buried under a pile of stuff. He'd have to resort to her bed, unless he was considering this very table.

'Do you have any sweet biscuits?'

'On the third shelf. There, under the yoghurt.'

Was he trying to reclaim some credit with her? No way could she sit at a table and drink tea with him as if everything was suddenly hunky-dory. Perhaps he felt the same, because while he sat down too he only half shared the table, his chair partly turned away as if he might need a quick escape. He bypassed the tea and biscuits altogether.

She warmed her ice-cold fingers on her cup. 'You don't drink tea?'

'Not just now. I'm not the one with the shakes.' His glance drifted to her mouth and his brows edged together.

She frowned too, wishing her lips wouldn't turn dry at the merest hint of—anything. 'Oh, that. It was nothing. Just a low blood sugar thing.'

Though, really, the tea was very welcome. She only gave the biscuit a token couple of nibbles. It was hard to eat with an interested protagonist seated directly opposite her. What if chocolate adhered to her lips?

Even though his eyes were veiled, her body was alert to his powerful masculine pull. Seemed as if all her nerves were crackling in awareness and it affected everything. Her breasts, her insides, her general steadiness.

It was the age-old problem. Intense physical attraction seemed designed to be unbearable. Surely that was a flaw in the blueprint?

It even occurred to her, watching his body language, that he was feeling the discomfort as keenly as she was. Good. Great. Let him suffer.

'That's better,' she said after a couple of gulps. 'Thanks. Anyway... It was really—good of you to intervene at the chopping block. You've bought me some breathing space, at least. I appreciate it. Thanks very much.'

He shrugged. 'My pleasure.' The edges of his sexy mouth curled up a little, and she tried not to think of how those lips had tasted. So firm, so warmly arousing and addictive. If things had been different...

*No.* Exile the thought. There'd be no biting of lips—gently or otherwise. No sexy little lip-tugs between lovers. This guy didn't do loving.

'Right,' he said authoritatively. Straightening his chair, he faced her directly, clasping his hands on the table before him. His dark brows edged together, his eyes taking on a serious focus. 'We need to start at once. Those jackals haven't given you much of a timeframe.'

'Sorry?'

He gestured. 'Planning. The campaign. Your ads for Fleur Elise.'

A dim understanding began to penetrate her fog. She widened her eyes in surprise. 'You mean you were serious about that?'

He blinked. 'Well, sure I was. What did you think? You've signed their agreement now. You have to do *something*. And fast. And, from my own point of view, my professional reputation is at stake here. Just think. More than thirty people are now witness to the fact that you and I have struck a deal. Luckily I've a little leeway with my schedule this month. We can get things underway right now or…' He appraised her with a glance, then looked at his watch. 'It might be best done over dinner. You can outline your operation for me, and the goals you've set.'

'*Goals?*' She lifted her brows. Heck. Goals. It wasn't that she was especially slow. Well, she probably was in a business sense. No, it was more that he was *fast*. Rushing her into things before she'd had time even to get used to the idea she was actually talking to him.

How the world had changed in a short time. Here he was, *in her kitchen*, when she'd resolved never even to think about him again.

'What are you saying? Heavens, I can't possibly accept *charity*. From y—anyone.' She went hot just thinking about it.

His eyes glinted. 'No. Course not. You are an O'Neill, after all.' His tone was gently mocking. 'But no need to panic the rugged old ancestors. I'm not offering charity. We'll do it strictly low-budget, using resources we already have. Then, once you start to turn a decent profit, you can pay me for any small costs that accrue along the way. It's my version of working *pro bono*.' He gave a ghost of a smile. 'Works for me. Okay?'

It sounded good. Maybe that was why her alarm bells were clanging. *Good* was too good to be true. What was in it for him? He had to have a motive. Everyone had a motive, it seemed. And his offer might not be one of charity, altogether, but whichever way she looked at it she'd owe him.

She couldn't help noticing he was looking far more relaxed now he'd switched into his ad man mode. Crisp. Bristling with confidence and know-how. Well, naturally. He had all the answers.

Whereas she… Did she want to be under an obligation to him?

He was studying her, reading her wariness, a wry twist to his mouth. 'You have two months, Amber. *Two months*. It isn't very long to mount a campaign. Most of ours take double or triple that in the planning, what with the research and the artistic work. This one will have to be realised in a matter of days. I'll have to snatch a few hours here, a few there—whatever I can fit in with my current schedule. If it's to work you'll have to open your mind to the possibilities and go with the flow.' He added softly, 'That's if you're serious about wanting to improve your shop's performance.'

'I am, of course. But…' It was no use. A massive elephant was towering between them and she couldn't continue to pretend it wasn't there. 'Are you *using* this situation? Does this have something to do with the other night?'

She met his eyes full-on. Though only for an instant. Because after that one charged instant he slid his away from her and screened them with his lashes.

His brow creased. A muscle shifted in his jaw then he said, so gruff his voice was a growl, 'Look…' He made a constrained gesture. 'About that. I understand I hurt your feelings. I regret it intensely. I'm honestly sorry if I made you feel…'

He appeared to be gazing through the glass at her mother's precious china teapot collection, but from the rigidity of his posture, the taut tendons in his bronzed neck, she doubted he was thinking about china.

'I'm ashamed to have bruised your feelings. I'm hoping we can put it behind us and forget it ever happened.'

A savage pang sliced through her. What with the pricking at the back of her eyes it took her a second to bring out an answer. Without the liberating fuel of anger, openly referring to the distressful matter wasn't easy. But at least there was some relief in recognising the ring of sincerity in his apology.

'Yes, well…' Her own voice was gruff. 'I suppose we can all be wrong. All right. We'll put it behind us.'

He glanced at her. 'Accept it was a mistake. All of it.'

She nodded, eyes lowered.

His voice was smoother. A little warmer. 'Maybe we both got carried away with excitement. Out of our comfort zones.'

She shrugged acquiescence. Of a sort. There had been some moments there when she'd been right within hers. Best not to revisit that. 'Let's just forget the whole thing.'

'Fine.' He frowned, serious and meditative, as sober as a bank manager. 'We'll write it off to experience, then. Deal?' He held out his hand.

Despite the managerial sobriety she noticed his eyes shimmer.

Manners warred with her instinct for self-preservation, and as usual self-preservation was the big-time loser.

'Deal, then.' She let him clasp her hand in his warm, firm grip.

*Oh, Amber. Mistake.* Fireworks sizzled up her arm and for a second or two her giddy brain couldn't quite remember what the deal was. Or the day. Or her name.

Though his mouth remained firm and cool, there was no concealing the silvery gleam in his irises. 'Great,' he said, straightening his shoulders, a new buoyancy in his tone. 'Right. We need to start planning ASAP. I'm thinking dinner—somewhere local to save time. I'll leave that with you, since you have the local knowledge. It'll be on me. Half an hour enough time?'

She hadn't been thinking about dinner—not with him at any rate. But, carried along on the flow of this sudden burst of crisp, authoritative energy, she nodded. Well, a girl had to eat. Whether or not she'd be able to swallow in his presence would be another story.

She supposed she could telescope her need to bathe, dress, work on her face and reflect deeply into half an hour.

He sprang to his feet and headed out with a brisk step, pausing to glance around at her as he fought his way through the obstacle path in the hall. 'Have you only just moved in here?'

'No, no. This stuff is only temporarily here. I needed to clear some space.'

'Ah.' He nodded, peering into the shadows of the sitting room. There wasn't enough moon yet for the skylight to make much difference. 'Space for what?'

'Well, it helps me to sleep sometimes if I dance.'

He turned to gaze at her, his brows elevated. *'Dance?'*

'That's correct.' She ignored the way his eyes lit up, as if she'd confessed to being a closet trapeze artist. She dampened her tone to keep it as flat and uninteresting as possible. 'I used to be a dancer. The exercise helps to relax me. Before I sleep.'

'Right. I see.' He moved to the door. Stood there with his back to her. 'That explains so much. Every time I've seen you I've thought… Er…' He cleared his throat and turned to her. In the short silence one of those moments of intense suspense gathered.

She waited—expectant, hardly breathing—then he lifted his eyes to hers. They were glittering, quite intense and sincere.

'About the other night. Well, I hope you *know* that at no time did I think you were anything but beautiful, gorgeous and exciting.'

The words swirled meaningless around in her head. All she *knew* was that her heart was bumping like crazy.

But she gave him a cool, repressive glance. 'Half an hour, then?'

She closed the door firmly after him.

# CHAPTER SEVEN

'I CAN'T believe I didn't guess.' Guy adapted his stride to fit Amber's. 'That first night we met. Remember? The pizza guy? You were wearing your ballet slippers then. You must have been dancing that night.'

She was leading him on a winding, undulating trek through residential streets down towards the harbour. Summery fragrances wafting from behind garden walls mingled with hers. She had on a violet dress in some soft fabric. Narrow straps pressed into the smooth, satin flesh of her shoulders.

He was careful not to brush her bare arm. Each time they passed under a streetlamp a different angle of her face was illuminated. His eye kept being magnetically drawn to look again. Her mouth. Her neck. Her mouth.

It felt good to be out with a woman. Chatting, even if it was a little strained. Seeing the world through feminine eyes. Not that this was anything like a date. Hell, no.

Banter was strictly off the menu. No flirting allowed. Looking was the most he could aspire to now. Unless there was a way to reassure her she could trust him to…what? Be more the sort of guy she could cuddle up to? Could he even trust himself?

'It wasn't the pizza guy who disturbed me.' She threw him a smiling look.

Aha, a smile. His blood quickened with pleasure and relief. A smile was the beginning of many a fantastic evening. He could do great things on the inspiration of a smile.

Sex, of course, was a no-go zone. He would have to stay well clear of the topic. Which was hard, what with sex and the art of the dance being so closely related. Interwined. Like lovers, one might say.

In response to her gentle gibe he covered his heart with mock humility. 'In my defence, Your Honour, I didn't think anyone was home.' He glanced at her, invigorated to a bit of over-recklessness on the strength of that smile. 'Do you always do it in the dark?'

Her lashes flickered down to make soft concealing arcs. He could have bitten his tongue off. Was he insane? Where was his control? He held his breath for fear he'd damaged the delicate accord.

But she ignored his witty *double entendre*. Maybe she hadn't even noticed.

'It isn't usually all that dark,' she said evenly. 'If there's a moon, the skylight makes the room bright enough. There isn't anywhere near enough space in there, of course, but it's my biggest room.'

He glanced at her once, then again. Her delicious lips were tightly pressed. She was wearing that expression. The one that froze him out. The snowball's chance in hell one. She'd noticed, all right.

He felt chagrin. No doubt he was a blundering fool, but eggshells had never been so precarious for walking on. If she didn't want him to continue desiring her, she shouldn't have told him she danced in the dark. What was *that* all about, anyway? And why tell a helpless visionary like him about it unless to enchant and seduce him?

'What I meant to *say* was…' He scrambled to right him-

# SAVE UP TO 25%

Subscribe to Modern today and get 4 books a month delivered to your door for 3, 6 or 12 months and gain up to 25% OFF! That's a fantastic saving of over £40!

| MONTHS | FULL PRICE | YOUR PRICE | SAVING |
|--------|-----------|-----------|--------|
| 3 | £41.88 | £35.61 | 15% |
| 6 | £83.76 | £67.02 | 20% |
| 12 | £167.52 | £125.64 | 25% |

As a welcome gift we will also send you a FREE L'Occitane gift set worth £10

**PLUS, by becoming a member you will also receive these additional benefits:**

🌸 FREE Home Delivery

🌸 Receive new titles TWO MONTHS AHEAD of the shops

🌸 Exclusive Special Offers & Monthly Newsletter

🌸 Special Rewards Programme

No Obligation - You can cancel your subscription at any time by writing to us at Mills & Boon Book Club, PO Box 676, Richmond. TW9 1WU.

To subscribe, visit
**millsandboon.co.uk/subscriptions**

P2G

self. 'What if there isn't a moon? Is there anything wrong with dancing in the light?'

Her voice was a little gruff. 'No. It's…' She hesitated, gave a shrug. 'Oh, well. I'm probably conscious of needing to save on the electricity bill. I try to go without using it wherever I can.' A flush suffused her cheek.

It slayed him. Call him a bleeding heart, but that small simple truth devastated him. It was so obvious. Why hadn't he realised? What an idiot he was. What a spoiled, complacent, *rich* idiot.

She glanced at him and added earnestly, 'Though there can be something really atmospheric about dancing in the dark. If the music is right. If you could imagine that.'

He could imagine it so vividly he could barely meet her eyes. He said constrainedly, 'I think I can. What sort of dancing do you do?'

'Well, I was with the Oz Ballet. Now I do a bit of everything. Whatever I get the chance to do.'

Didn't he just know it?

'Wow,' he said. 'The Australian Ballet. That's really impressive. That's like being an Olympic champion.'

She gave him an ironic look meant to convey his crassness in not understanding the difference between sport and art.

And it was just, to some degree. His imagination was hooked on her gymnastic ability. On a piano. Her lithe and lovely form folding into a flower. Then unfolding. Into a woman. Driving him wild.

Wicked, witty lines he might have used to remind her of that moment rose to his tongue, but regretfully he had to restrain them. All forbidden, alas. He must behave as though he'd never touched her. Never tasted her mouth or sunk himself into her silken flesh.

'Oh.' She lifted her head. 'Looks like it's pretty busy. I hope they kept our table.'

Following the direction of her gaze, he entered a surreal moment. Of all things, his bemused gaze assured him, she was leading him to a church. Set on a grassy knoll overlooking the harbour, with its pretty spire and stained glass lit invitingly from within, it looked charming enough to attract a swarm of unbelievers.

But not Guy Wilder. Never him.

His heart went stone-cold.

'You mean we're eating *here*?' He halted abruptly, hardly knowing what he said. 'This is it?'

She nodded, beaming up at him. 'I know. Isn't it gorgeous? I've always wanted to try it. They say the cuisine is quite authentic.'

Guy barely heard. Must have been the shock. Before he could stop it the last fateful time he'd stood in a church rolled right back to sandbag him in full vivid Technicolor.

Flowers. Everywhere flowers. All of their friends, even his parents. The priest, gorgeous in her celebratory robes. Violet edged with gold. He'd concentrated on them while he waited. Colours for festivity. Joy. Her encouraging smiles beginning to wear a bit thin. More waiting. An eternity of waiting.

Relentless minutes ticking by. Murmurings. The bride was late, someone said. Ridiculously late, surely? He'd begun to wonder himself.

The suspense. In his nerves. In the air. And the restlessness he'd suddenly started to sense. Little rustlings amongst the congregation. Murmurs.

His hands had suddenly been damp, his beautifully laundered collar uncomfortably tight. His man's finery wilting. But he'd stood upright, sure and confident, trusting to the end. Though others around him were giving in, twisting to scan the long, empty aisle.

The anguished look he'd caught between a couple of his mates… It had confused him, while at the same time cutting him to the quick. What were they thinking? And then the moment. That gut-wrenching moment when he'd understood.

All at once he felt the weight of Amber O'Neill's clear gaze. He realised his hands were clenched. With an effort he dragged himself back to the here and now.

Hell, it was nothing to do with her. Amber wasn't to know what a fool he'd been made. Made of himself. He wasn't a madman, for goodness' sake. Just the common or garden variety of lunatic who'd entrusted a piece of himself to a woman.

The church had come as a surprise, that was all. But it was a restaurant. Only a restaurant.

'Guy?' She looked concerned. 'Are you all right? You look so grim all of a sudden.'

'Yeah?' Deliberately he made his muscles and everything inside him unclench. He breathed normally and flashed her a grin. 'Must be hunger. You know that low blood sugar thing?'

Amber smiled, though uncertainly. Grim had been too mild a word for what she'd imagined. For a second there she'd imagined something almost stark in his expression, though there was no sign of it now. Still, she'd heard the note of surprise in his voice when he'd spotted the restaurant.

A dismaying thought struck her. What if he couldn't afford it? Since this was only meant to be a discussion about the shop, maybe he'd intended a café or somewhere more simple.

Had she blundered with her choice?

Though he seemed too well dressed for a café, looking so groomed and sleek. Not that she was looking. Or smelling. All the way here she'd made a point of *not*. She'd deliberately kept her hand from brushing his sleeve and kept her eyes fixed on the path ahead. Though it was impossible not to notice the smoothness of his lean cheek. Clearly he'd shaved for the occasion, because she remembered how he'd looked beforehand. Vividly. And he smelled quite— woodsy.

Probably not like the Wessex woods, of course, where Eustacia Vye was wont to roam. When she wasn't stalking Kirribilli like a cat on a hot tin roof.

'Look, Guy,' she said. 'This place looks a lot more expensive than I realised. It's probably a bit up-market for a business discussion. But I'm pretty sure we can still cancel.' She dug for her mobile. 'There are plenty of other places.'

His expression lightened. 'Hey—no, no. Put that away.' His strange mood, if it had ever been there, vanished without a trace. 'Here will be fine. Honestly. You're my client, and the client must be properly wooed.' His grin was reassuring. 'Up-market is how we do biz at Wilder Solutions.'

'Is it really?' Amber wasn't altogether convinced. But, however Wilder Solutions chose to operate, she felt honour-bound to pay her share.

She resolved not to eat much. If she ordered the cheapest dish on the menu it would keep costs down. This wasn't an occasion for the letting down of hair, anyway. She'd be keeping hers tightly bound up.

In fact it would certainly be unwise to accept wine, should Guy suggest it. She wondered if a French restaurant would be likely to serve vee juice. It was important to remember how reckless she'd been on the night of the wine. Not that the wine had been totally to blame. Other things had been in play then.

The music. His hands. His mouth.

As though to mock her, as soon as she stepped inside the gothic portal the ripple of a piano slunk into her ears. An old lovesong with a haunting refrain. The old black magic slithered wickedly along Amber's veins, inevitably bringing to mind her late erotic adventures.

She could have groaned. Why did she have to be so susceptible? That 'adventure' had had serious consequences to her peace of mind. Ignoring the liquid tones tugging at her heartstrings, she steadfastly resisted looking at Guy. The last thing she wanted to do was remind him. Something told her any references to that night would be dangerous in the extreme.

The trouble was it was reminding *her*. This tight rein of control she was attempting to exert on her primitive instincts needed to be yanked tighter and tighter. Why did the senses have to overrule everything? The more she saw of Guy, even with what she'd learned, the more alive she was to his appeal.

It seemed their sexual exchange was branded on her body's memory. A barrier had been removed and, though a different one was in place, the lack of the first was having a weakening effect.

If she wasn't careful, before she knew it she'd be crawling up on that piano lid.

He was glancing around him, taking in the fittings. 'Well, it doesn't *feel* like a church. Doesn't sound like one either.'

He smiled, but she pretended not to understand his meaning. Before he could make any other sly references to recent history she said, 'Not with all those delicious aromas coming from the kitchen. Mmm… Smell the garlic.'

The place was abuzz, with waiters swishing adroitly between tables and bearing steaming dishes. The tantalising fragrances made Amber's stomach juices yearn. Lucky her years of ballet training hadn't been for nothing. In the food department, at least, she could do abstinence standing on her head.

As she approached their table, conscious of Guy behind her, she felt his light touch in the small of her back. Just the standard polite, masculine touch. Instantly a tiny electric tingle shimmied up her spine and infected her blood.

She settled into her place, lashes lowered. That quickening in her blood and the warm tidal surge to her breasts was too pleasant a sensation to quell all at once. But, tempting though it might have been to meet Guy's eyes, it was important not to. She had to keep her focus on the shop. The meeting. Not on his hands. Not on his mouth.

He slipped off his jacket and hung it on his chair. Impossible not to glance at least once. His linen shirt, white against his tan, was cut with a casual elegance that suited his lean build. Perfect for the warm evening. His sinewy forearms, those hands, would have tempted a nun's eyes to linger, but she made herself look away while the image burned in her retina.

She needed to remember. Though grateful for his apology, and respectful of it, it couldn't essentially change what she'd learned about him. About how much he was prepared to offer another soul. During the midnight hours, when the need for human comfort was at its most searing.

When the sommelier arrived and Guy suggested champagne or a cocktail she politely declined and enquired about juice.

'Very wise,' Guy said as the waiter took her modest order. 'We need to keep our wits about us.'

But she noticed that for himself he ordered a glass of

champagne. Watching it foam into his glass, so zingy and alive, she couldn't help thinking how refreshing it looked. Guy savoured his first sip like a connoisseur, closing his eyes in a sort of ecstasy.

She couldn't restrain herself from commenting. 'Anyone would think it was nectar.'

'That's what it reminds me of.' He held the flute high, the better to appreciate the wine's pallid sparkle. 'The divine nectar of the lotus. Would you like a taste?' His eyes shimmered into hers, enticement in their depths.

'No, thanks.'

What did he mean by bringing up the lotus, anyway? Was it some sort of sly jab about the other night? She retreated to her carrot juice. Tried not to notice how flat it was. How thick and pointless. But tonight abstinence was her middle name. So when it came time to order the food she remained wedded to her resolve.

'I'll just have a green salad, thank you.'

The waiter, a small dramatic man with a not-very-convincing French accent, seemed mortally wounded by her restraint.

Guy was even harder to convince. He stared at her above the top of his menu and his black brows shot up. 'Truly? Is that all?'

She reached for her juice. 'That's all I require, thanks.'

He studied her, his head a little to one side. A gleam crept into his eyes. He glanced at the waiter, then back at his menu, his brow wrinkling. 'Hmm…I'm tempted by the *potage*, myself, but I'm not entirely sure how substantial onion soup is likely to be. So for my entrée, along with my soup, I'll order the duck parfait with balsamic onion jam and cornichons, and the cheese and walnut soufflé with frisée and pear salad.'

'All for *monsieur*?' The waiter could scarcely keep the shock from his voice. 'While *mademoiselle* goes hungry?'

Guy nodded gravely, though his eyes danced with amusement. '*Mademoiselle* prefers to dine lightly, while I find myself ravenous. For my main course I'll have the Châteaubriand with the mushroom ragout, witlof salad, Dutch carrots and Pommes Lyonnaise.'

A look of sly triumph occupied the waiter's face. 'Aha. It *desolates* me to inform *monsieur* that the Châteaubriand is only permitted for two diners. If you read on further, you will see there is a single-serve dish of *filet* with Brussels sprouts and a lentil *jus. Very* substantial—even for such a hungry man as yourself.'

Guy shook his head. 'I don't think so. I'm not much of a Brussels sprouts man. I'm afraid I have my heart set on the Châteaubriand.'

Amber nearly gasped. Was the man a glutton?

The waiter shared her concern. 'But, *monsieur*. This Châteaubriand is a very *large dish.*' He demonstrated excitedly with both hands. 'There are two platters and side dishes to accompany. The Pommes Lyonnaise alone…' He threw up histrionic hands as though words failed him.

'I find I have a very large appetite,' Guy said. 'In fact, I see here in your *dégustation* menu you suggest a wine to accompany each individual dish.'

The waiter's brows shot high on his forehead. He said incredulously, '*Monsieur* is wishing to order different wines with *each individual dish*?'

Guy frowned. 'Oh, hang on there. Not *every* wine. Just this *sauv blanc*. And yes. I think the Bordeaux. The Châteaubriand deserves the finest available red, don't you think? And bring the rest of this bottle, will you?'

He indicated the champagne. Rolling his eyes, the

waiter departed, but soon the bottle was produced and placed in a *très* elegant ice bucket.

Amber eyed Guy bemusedly. Surely he wouldn't drink all that, and then *more*? The man would be sloshed. How much planning would get done?

She watched him pour himself more champagne from the bottle and raise it to his lips. As he savoured the sip, a strange expression crept over his face. 'I'm not sure this is the same wine.' He examined the label, sniffed it thoughtfully, then sipped again. 'Nope. If it *is* the same it's from a different bottle. This stuff's off.'

'*Off*? Are you sure?' She glanced about at the austere gloss of the exclusive place. Every surface gleamed with class and honour. 'What do you mean? Surely they wouldn't—? Not *here*.'

He gave a solemn nod. 'I'm afraid it can happen anywhere. If you don't believe me…here, look. Give me that glass. Tell me if this tastes sour and vinegary to you.'

She handed over her empty water glass and he poured her a substantial drop of champagne. 'Now, try that. Tell me if you think the quality has been compromised.'

Conscious of his grey gaze sparkling with alertness, she took a cautious sip. After the carrot juice, the wine tasted pleasantly tart on her tongue. Swallowing was like drinking a delicious mouthful of ocean wave. Almost as soon as the zesty bubbles hit her stomach streams of sensuous warmth irradiated her middle.

'What do you think?' There was a veiled gleam in Guy's eyes, his crow's feet charmingly apparent.

She glanced at him from under her lashes. 'I can't really tell yet.'

Well, it was essential to conduct a test rigorously. These French champagnes didn't come cheap.

If Ivy could see her now…

If Ivy had read the prices on this menu…

She smiled. 'I think perhaps the carrot juice could still be affecting my palate. I could probably give you a more accurate reading next time.' She held out her glass. 'A little more, please.'

This time she closed her eyes and swirled the blessed drop on her tongue before swallowing. 'Mmm. Oh yes, *yes*. A little tangy to start with. Creamy. And then you get the full surge effect. And what a fantastic climax. *Bliss*.'

Heavens. Her eyes flew open. Had she actually *said* that, or just thought it?

He was scrutinising her, and with that silvery shimmer in his eyes, and the almost-smile curling up the corners of his mouth, she had the impression she might have actually said it.

'So?' he said, as smoothly as a wolf emerging from the trees of the Wessex woods. 'What's the verdict?'

She smiled. Gave a small bewitching laugh. 'Don't think I don't know your game. You did that deliberately. You're devious, Guy Wilder.' She shoved her glass across the table at him. 'Go on, then. Fill it up.'

It would have been unreasonable to drink his wine and then refuse to participate in any of the feast when it was delivered. Whether by art or coincidence, Guy found he didn't really care for soufflé after all, or onion soup. He finagled a swap with her green salad, yet somehow she ended up eating as much of it as he did. As for the Châteaubriand, her half was sublime, especially washed down with a drop of Bordeaux.

And it was only a tiny drop. She wasn't entirely seduced by the wine. But by the man…?

She was grappling with that. Desire seemed to burn more fiercely when emerging from under a cloud. Her

memories of his lips and hands on her body were powerful enough. The glow in his eyes seared her to the marrow.

As if by mutual accord neither she nor Guy made any
reference to past wounds inflicted. Somehow, over des-
sert, he managed to listen to her dreams about the shop
without laughing. And on the way home, after she'd tucked
a copy of the menu into her purse to show Ivy, she must
have forgotten for the moment who she was talking to—
because she told him all about her mother.

He kept nodding and looking very grave, asking her
things about Lise when she'd been well and strong, as
if she was still a person worth discussing. Strange as it
might seem, it was a relief to talk about her mother as a
woman who'd lived and loved and achieved things. It was
as though Guy understood about losing someone.

Strolling along moonlit streets after an evening replete
with fine food, wine and more than a few laughs made
conversation the safest option. And strangely, even after
her ordeal earlier in the evening—or maybe because of
it—it didn't feel so weird to share things with him.

One good thing a fling achieved was to break the ice,
she reflected. Especially a failed fling. There was no point
holding back on the family skeletons when people already
knew the worst about each other.

'Coming home to nurse your mother was a great thing
to do,' he said. 'But what about your career? When will
you take that up again?'

She dropped her gaze. 'Well… That's pretty well over
now. My place in the company has been given away long
since.' She made a rueful grimace. 'Lucky I've got the
shop. Now I'm a businesswoman. At least being so bright
green I fit in with the stock.'

She laughed, and he smiled along with her, though soon
she noticed him frowning to himself.

'What about you?' she said, eager to shrug off the subject of the shop for once. 'Where are your parents?'

He made a laconic face. 'Around. Last I heard they were in Antarctica.'

She glanced at him in surprise. 'Don't you keep in touch?'

'Not very often.' He shrugged. 'They're scientists. They do *vaguely* know they've got a son somewhere, I think.'

She chuckled. 'So they do remember?'

'Mostly. But their focus is saving the planet.' He flashed her an ironic grin. 'You can hardly blame them. There are far more fascinating specimens than this.' He spread his arms to indicate himself.

She wasn't so sure of that. He had her full attention.

She gazed at him in disbelief. 'How long has this gone on?'

'Always. I guess you'd say my grandfather had the pleasure of raising me while they gadded about the globe.'

'Oh, no!' she exclaimed, not sure whether or not his amused description concealed resentment. 'Aren't you angry with them?'

He shook his head. 'Not really. It probably seemed sensible not to keep dragging me out of school. My grandfather was a great old guy.' He smiled in recollection. 'Always had something to laugh about.'

'Oh.' She lifted her brows. 'So…your grandfather… is he…?'

He nodded. 'Yep. Couple of years ago, now. That's partly why I find myself holed up in Jean's flat. Not solely to annoy Amber O'Neill and keep her awake.' The moonlight picked up the silvery gleam in his eyes. 'My grandfather left me his house and I've been renovating it. I've done a lot of it myself, but now it's at that tricky stage where you have to call in the professionals.'

Maybe *she* was at a tricky stage.

The evening air felt unusually warm, almost languorous on her skin. Other couples might have been tempted to take advantage of the occasional shadowy niches between garden walls to indulge in a sexy clinch.

But not her and Guy. She sensed his desire, though. Every lingering glance from his darkened eyes burned. And every longing nerve cell told her he was as alive to the conditions as she was herself. If he once touched her...

She walked carefully, so as not to brush his sleeve with her hand. 'I'm sorry about your grandfather. Do you miss him?'

He nodded. 'I guess. I think of him often. Things he said.' He smiled at her. 'What about you?' His brows edged together. 'I can't get over what a sacrifice you've made, leaving your career like that.'

She wanted to cover her ears. He shouldn't be sympathising with her, tugging at her old desires like that. Heaven knew, she was weak enough to give in to self-pity over the way her life had turned out without being given more encouragement.

'Look,' she said firmly, 'it's not as noble as it sounds. I never intended to totally abandon it. That was just how it turned out. Gradually, over time. I took leave from the company in pieces—whenever there was a crisis. A few weeks here, a few there. I always expected Mum to get well. In the end I realised I was causing the company problems, so I resigned.'

'But surely they'd take you back? Surely?'

She looked hesitantly at him. All her doubts and anxieties crowded into her mind. Would she even be up to it now? Eighteen months was a long time to go without full daily rehearsal. 'But I have the shop now. I'm fine.'

He didn't look convinced. Kept searching her face, frowning. 'Where's your old man in all this?'

'Nowhere.' She grimaced. 'He left us when I was a kid. Flew to LA for a business conference, never to be seen or heard from again.'

He glanced sharply at her. 'Is that right? Never again? Didn't he ever contact your mother?'

'I suppose he must have, because they did divorce finally. I guess I didn't really know all that went on between them. Just the days Mum looked weepy and upset.'

'Life's hard, isn't it?' He walked in silence for a while, frowning. Then said quietly, 'She must have been devastated.'

'Oh, she was. After a while, though, she kept saying it was for the best. He was never going to grow up.'

That silence lasted for minutes. She couldn't help thinking how amazing it was to be talking to Guy like this. Maybe she should give herself a good pinch. Her feelings about him over the last couple of days had been so negative.

While tonight he seemed so accessible. Gorgeous. Though initially the other night he'd been warm, too. And gorgeous before the sex. Was she being a fool? Being sucked in again by easy charm and that pulse that kept drawing her to him like an electromagnet?

They were in the street that led to the arcade when he asked, 'Do you think if he'd asked to come back she'd have given him another chance?'

She looked quickly at him. Where had that come from? But she couldn't read his eyes. 'I doubt it. I saw how hurt she was. How—shattered. Humiliated in every sense. Once your illusions have been destroyed…'

'Yeah.' There was heartfelt agreement in that single low syllable.

He didn't speak again until they were in the lift, where vibrations between them seemed to intensify.

'How about you, Amber?' Though his voice sounded casual, the darkened eyes on her face were intent. 'Would you have given him a second chance?'

Her heart skidded. The subtext was clear now. He was talking about her and him. Would she give him another chance? Another chance to make love to her.

She knew what her body yearned for her to say. The temptation to touch him was extreme. But pride, self-esteem or whatever else forced her to hold her nerve.

'I'd have needed to be convinced, Guy.'

A muscle twitched in his cheek. 'What would you expect? A preview?'

'A reasonable explanation would be a start.'

Frowning, he dragged a hand through his hair. The air tautened with suspense, with an almost tangible sense of his reluctance. Each time his darkened gaze clashed with hers the intensity in his glance dragged at her breasts and turned her insides to liquid.

When they reached her door she paused, hoping against hope he would say something. *Anything* to revive her illusions.

'Well…' Her voice was husky with night fever. 'That was a lovely dinner. Thank you. It was good to—talk.'

He remained silent, his mouth compressed to a firm straight line.

She added, 'I feel as if we understand each other a bit better.'

His jaw set hard.

'Which is good, if we're to work together.'

There was nothing more to say, so she turned to unlock her door.

'Amber.'

His deep voice interrupted her as she inserted her key. She faced him again.

'I…' He lifted his arms from his sides and let them fall again. 'I haven't taken a woman out in a while.' Unwilling at the start, the words finished in a rush.

Her ears pricked up, her heart tensing with thrilled anticipation. 'Really?'

'No.'

She waited for more, but he didn't add anything. Just stood looking like a rock that had reluctantly squeezed out a precious drop of its lifeblood.

She lifted her brows. 'Is that *it*?'

He drew an exasperated breath. 'Look, I don't *talk* about all that relationship palaver. It's just that you might as well know I had a—' He swung away to evade her eyes. 'A break-up, I suppose you'd call it, with a woman a while back, and I've probably been avoiding all the—stuff.'

'The stuff?' she mused aloud, though inside her spirit was doing cartwheels at having commanded such a grand achievement. 'And what would that be, I wonder? The *stuff*?'

His eyes glinted and he took her arms in a firm grip. 'You're just loving this, aren't you? You think you've got the power.'

She gave one of those tinkling little laughs. But it was filled with excitement, fuelled by the thrilling sensation of electricity tingling where his skin collided with hers. 'Don't be silly. As if women ever think about power.'

He gave a brief sardonic laugh. Then his expression lightened. 'I don't suppose you'll be dancing tonight?'

A sliver of excitement shot down her spine. 'Probably. After everything today, I might have to.'

'Ah. Do you know…' the gleam in his eyes intensified '…I'd really love to see that?'

# CHAPTER EIGHT

AMBER had changed into a simple white dress with a hem that floated around her knees. Guy could see through the flimsy fabric to something white she had on underneath.

What he was about to witness was the real thing, he realised, taking in her preparations with a weird thrill down his spine. A sense of how lucky he was, how *privileged* to be allowed into something so essentially private, gave him a pang of misgiving. What if he blew it again? What if he said the wrong thing and somehow bruised her feelings?

She was right, though, about the atmosphere without electric light. The moon filled the room with a ghostly glow, reflected in the wall mirrors she'd placed at either end. Along the third wall she had an empty bookcase turned on its side to serve as her *barre*.

When she moved across the room to the stereo his anticipation sharpened into suspense. She touched something, then the opening chords of 'Clair de Lune' shimmered on the air.

He held his breath.

Gliding to stand under the skylight, she extended her arms upwards. Then, after casting him a long, mysterious glance, she started. She rose on her toes and reached up to the moon and danced—a spirit of the night in thrall to the music. She seemed possessed by some elemental magic. It was spellbinding, every movement perfection, every line of her graceful form lovely.

As she swooped down, then reached up to glide and twirl gently on her toes, the moonlight turned her skin translucent and caught a faint lustre in her dress. Once or twice she sent him another of those long, galvanising glances. It was so—intimate. Almost confiding. He felt as if she was inviting him in to share her experience.

His heart hammered like a schoolboy's.

He sat motionless on top of the pile on the sofa in the hall, mesmerised, hardly daring to breathe for fear of breaking the spell. Never in his life had he expected to be affected by *ballet*.

But the purity and simplicity of her movements, so expressive of the music, enslaved him.

As the last note faded he sat frozen, moved to his soul.

She turned to look at him. He could see the rise and fall of her breasts from her exertion, then he realised with shame his initial fascination in the whole business had been sensual. Still was, of course, on some level. Face it, *every* level. But the reality had been so much more than that.

'Amber…' His voice sounded as if it had issued from the centre of the earth.

Smiling at the crack in his voice, she strolled across to the stereo in her ballet slippers and switched it off. Half turning to deliver him an apologetic shrug, she said, 'It'd be better if I had more space.'

He clambered down from his perch. 'Oh, no,' he said, striding across to her, feeling like a great, hulking clumsy brute. 'No, it couldn't be better. It was…'

He was breathing so hard his insides might have been shaking. Faced with her gorgeous eager face, her eyes shining with comprehension of his appreciation, he felt his best words desert him.

He took her in his arms. 'Amber, I… Really, I…'

He couldn't help it. He risked everything and kissed her. Thank the gods or angels or whatever, she melted her soft, yielding curves against his hungry, burning bones and kissed him right back, her wine-sweet mouth so luscious, so arousing, he was instantly harder than a log.

He drew her lips into his mouth, glorying in their soft, addictive resilience. Her honeyed breath mingled with his, tongue tips touching. When the intoxicating event finally ended, to his extreme relief she took his hand and led him into her bedroom.

Exhilarated after her dance, and drunk with the kiss, Amber turned to face him, her veins ablaze with fever. Excitement made her tremble.

He dropped his jacket on the floor, then opened both hands before him. 'I'm crazy for you. But are you sure that you want this?'

Even if she hadn't read the faint sheen on his forehead, the tension apparent in his muscles, there was an intensity in his voice that spoke of his desire.

She moved close and placed her hand flat over his heart. She could feel the big muscle under her palm. Thumping like crazy, all right. Like her own.

'Oh, I want it,' she said, breathless in her heartfelt sincerity. 'Want you.'

He kissed her again fiercely, possessively, pushing her up against a wall, his big hot hands seeking the fastenings of her dress while he pinned her with his pelvis and ground his hips against her.

She could feel the hard bulk of his erection against her abdomen. The friction was great, but it only made her sex burn with more need. She parted her thighs and hooked a leg around him, the better to rub her maddened flesh against that seductive ridge.

'Rock me, rock me,' she rasped, her body yearning for contact of the sexy, masculine kind.

'Steady now,' he warned. 'Not so fast.'

Though he seemed unable to take his own advice. He devoured her with kisses and caresses, including obligingly stroking that delicate spot with his fingers through the thin covering of her body stocking. She clung to him, moaning as waves of liquid pleasure thrilled through her aroused flesh.

The incredible friction was fantastic, but only served to increase the burning demand inside her.

Thirsting for total skin contact, she helped him find the fastenings to her dress. She could feel the heat in his urgent hands as he lowered the zip, interspersing every small act with more hot, greedy kisses. Her face, her throat, her breasts.

'I could eat you alive,' he breathed with husky fervour. 'You're gorgeous. So beautiful. So—so everything.'

The dress fell to the floor and the body stocking soon followed. Amber bent to untie her slippers.

'No, leave them a minute,' he commanded. 'I want to— look at you.'

Breathing hard, he reached a hand to stroke her, tracing a gentle line from shoulder to hip, as if she were made of some rare and precious material.

The dark flame in his eyes burned. 'You know, I never expected to be with you again.' His voice had that deep, gravelly quality.

Her heart lurched. Was he mocking her for her turn-around?

'You didn't want to be?' She searched his face.

He took a moment to answer. 'I was a fool. I thought I'd ruined my chances with you.'

She saw the seriousness in his eyes and realised there was no mockery.

'Well…' Her voice sank to a whisper. 'Things can change.'

He was silent, shadows she couldn't read coming and going in his expression.

She stepped forward and put her lips to his throat. At the same time her nimble fingers released his shirt buttons. Hungry for more of his salty, alluring *man* taste, she pushed his shirt aside and explored his muscled chest with her hands and lips.

He put his arms around her and kissed her lips, his chest hair grazing her breasts. Then, seized by a mutual urgency, each of them went for his belt buckle, excited hands colliding.

When at last he stood naked Amber's eyes widened in awe. 'Heavens.'

His penis was so thick and engorged, pulsing with the urgent life, she was nearly overcome. In rapturous worship she went down on her knees, held the marvellous creature in both hands and licked the salty tip.

He shuddered and let out a wild groan. Amazingly, his length thickened and grew harder in her hands.

'I suppose this must be quite tender here?' With a grin she closed her lips over the end and gave a mischievous little suck.

Guy tensed, making a quick move to quell the delicious procedure before it catapulted him too far, too soon. 'Hey—no way,' he bit out. 'Amber.' He pushed her away from his too-willing shaft, shaking his head with mock sternness. 'You could live to regret that.' Without ceremony he hauled her to her feet and thrust her onto the bed.

With a giggle at his expression, Amber lolled in luxurious anticipation of his next move. 'You're being very bossy.'

'That's because, sweetheart, right here and right now I *am* the boss.'

'Promise?' She fluttered her lashes. 'I admit I'm finding you really quite—dictatorial. I shudder to think what you might do to me.'

'Here,' he said, smiling, 'give me that foot.'

She lifted the foot and playfully wiggled it at him. He caught it, and with eyes gleaming untied the strings and peeled off her slipper.

'Aha,' he said, taking her foot in his big, warm hands.

It felt so pleasant, having her foot held. Comforting, even.

'There's magic in this pretty foot.'

He undressed the other foot, then kissed her toes and kneaded her soles with his thumbs. Guy's touch was far more exciting than the physio's at the ballet company. Her very soles felt aroused.

But what he did with the backs of her knees was pure devilry.

'Oh, yes,' she cried at the sensations tingling up her leg. 'There. *There*.'

Breaking from her, he bent down to where his clothes lay on the floor and searched. Then he sat on the side of the bed and sheathed himself.

Leaning up on an elbow to watch the operation, she observed with a smile. 'Well, well. I see you came prepared. In *spite* of your misgivings.'

He cast her a gleaming glance. 'And aren't you glad I'm an ever hopeful, upbeat kinda guy, even against all odds?'

'Oh, I'm glad, all right. I'm celebrating.' She giggled and kicked her legs high.

She was feeling so deliciously high and aroused, it occurred to her that what she was experiencing right here and now was happiness. Guy Wilder was *sorry*, still gorgeous, and here they both were. Against all the odds.

He stretched out beside her and took her in his arms. Then he kissed her lips. When he drew back, his eyes were warm and tender. 'You're making me feel so good I want to do something for you.'

'Oh, yeah?' She was suddenly breathless. 'What sort of thing?' Though she might be studying him cagily, the truth was she was eager. Wildly eager.

His eyes brimmed with amused comprehension and desire. 'Roll over,' he instructed, and when she complied he groaned with a conviction that was truly flattering, 'Oh, this gorgeous peach of a behind. I've dreamed of this.'

She was happy for him to enjoy her behind, or any other part that took his fancy. So when he started kissing the insides of her knees, and continued a fiery journey to the silky skin inside her thighs, divining where he might be headed, she co-operated with every move in a mounting ecstasy of hope and suspense.

And she wasn't disappointed. Soon his clever fingers were lighting tingling little fires as he stroked the highly aroused and sensitive skin of her bottom.

And *then*, thank the Lord, they slipped between her legs to softly massage the burning folds of her feminine mound.

'Ohh…' She sighed in helpless bliss, lifting her hips a little to accommodate the fabulous friction.

Time slowed. The temperature in the room skyrocketed. There was no sound but the rasp of their breathing, her moans, and her heart booming in her ears. Then softly, tenderly, Guy Wilder put his mouth between her legs and sucked. Creating the most intense and trembling rapture she could ever remember experiencing, he licked her sweetest, most intimate spot with his tongue.

Streams of intense delight irradiated her flesh. Blissful sensations swelled inside her like the sun on a spring morn, building and building to an irresistible, ever-beckoning pinnacle, and then when they were too much to endure, bursting into a thousand glorious rays of pleasure.

And that was only the beginning.

Amber O'Neill was floating. It felt so fantastic to be made love to. To share passion with a lover who laughed one minute, then in the next moved her heart unutterably.

'You're the real thing, aren't you?' he said at one point.

Bemused, she gazed at him. 'The real…*woman*?'

He laughed. 'Oh, no worries there. No, I mean…' His grin faded. 'You're a genuine ballerina. Do you do all the stuff? Swans and everything?'

She nodded, trying not to grin at his enthusiasm. 'Sugar plum fairies, princesses, firebirds—I do them all. Though swans are my specialty.'

His voice thickened. 'I'd love to see that.'

She smiled, though she didn't say what she thought. *I doubt you ever will.* Instead she said casually, 'You can come to see me at the Spanish club doing flamenco some Saturday evening, if you like.'

There were few long heartbeats. Then he said, 'I *would* like.'

And then there was that amazing moment when he entered her with one searing, virile thrust. He gazed down at her, his eyes fierce and at the same time so tender her heart shook.

'I never thought I could have this again with another woman.'

Questions sprang up in her mind, but were soon discarded as he took her higher than high, making love to her in every which way, bringing her to multiple orgasms, holding back on his own pleasure until at last, hot, hard and convincing, he reached his own shuddering climax.

After that, she slept in his arms.

# CHAPTER NINE

'WE'LL need a few flowers. All right?'

Guy swept in mid-morning, smiling and charged with plans, his eyes still warm from the night before. The several nights before. Up to thirteen now, by Amber's counting. Nights of sampling the local eating houses, cooking in Amber's kitchen, making out in the cinema, enjoying long and voluptuous lovemaking in Amber's bed.

Not that any evening ever started out that way. No definite plans were ever made. It always seemed just to happen that, whenever Amber was wondering if she would see Guy that night, by accident, and often in the most casual way, she'd bump into him somewhere. Then, before she knew it, things escalated and passion was the outcome.

It was fun to speculate how 'accidental' those heavenly meetings were. The ones she didn't engineer herself, that was. Though the L word hadn't been used, some beautiful things had been said, and her fingers were perpetually crossed.

This particular Tuesday morning she felt especially chirpy. Guy had phoned her soon after nine from his office. Something in his schedule had been delayed, he'd told her, so the crew had a timeslot to spare for Fleur Elise.

At last. Amber had been beginning to wonder if it would ever happen.

But today was all go, and she was bubbling with excitement. He was taking her to meet his team, and if they could come up with some satisfactory props, and the weather held, they might even start actual shooting. Outdoors, he told her they'd decided, as a cost-cutting measure. And, as another way to reduce costs, Guy seemed to think *she* could be the model for her own ad.

She kept grinning, imagining herself on camera. It wouldn't be the same as being on stage, of course, but shooting with Guy would be better than going over the accounts. Doing *anything* with Guy was better than anything else she could think of.

Amber had begged Ivy to come in and help the customers while Serena worked on the bouquets. She'd guessed Ivy would be eager, and Ivy was. Any opportunity to be running the show without Amber getting in the way was her bonus.

For once Amber didn't care. Oh, joyous day. She could *escape*.

Not that she didn't love her shop. She was absolutely grateful to have it. Especially when Guy breezed in, exuding energy and purpose. Everything glowed then.

Including her heart when he strolled up to her at her counter.

'How are you feeling?' He held her in his gaze as if she was the only woman in the world.

It was only a few hours since they'd been in each other's arms.

Amber had realised both Serena and Ivy had guessed about their connection. Ivy had accused her of being besotted. Amber didn't care if the whole world knew. She was happy, though she felt relieved that Guy understood that here in the shop there could be no touching. He was such an intuitive, professional, reliable, sensitive, gorgeous guy.

'Ready to be a star?' he added, his eyes gleaming.

'You'd better believe it.' It would have been churlish to mention she'd already tasted stardom for a couple of glorious years. 'And I feel—fantastic.' She used her husky voice. 'How about you?'

'Fan—tastic.'

And he looked it. Even with Ivy hovering nearby over a potential customer, and Serena poking her head out from the bunching room, flashing Amber grins and thumbs up, it was impossible *not* to eat him with her eyes.

He was in jeans today, though not the scruffy ones. These were more the sleek type preferred by movie directors and Italian racing car drivers. A crisp white shirt with the sleeves rolled back exposed the tanned desirability of his arms. Arms that had held her through the night. Arms she'd have stepped into right then and there if they'd been alone.

His gleaming grey gaze travelled over her outfit, reinforcing her pleasant inner blaze. 'Look at you. You're inspiring my vision. You look gorgeous.'

She smiled. 'And you look—edible.'

For some reason he wanted her in one of her work outfits to meet his team, so she hadn't changed from her satiny floral sheath. In shades of blue and lavender, with a hint of turquoise, it was shortish, and looked good with her one and only pair of four-inch heels. As well, she'd swirled her hair into a chignon and stuck in an iris.

Considering the last time he'd seen her she'd been naked apart from a sheet, she was glad she'd flowered up. Flowery had its advantages. It was hard not to look pretty when smothered in blooms.

Ivy bustled over, to elbow Amber out of the way so she could ring up a transaction, and Guy sharpened up his conversation for Ivy's benefit.

'It'll be good for the team to see you in your workwear,' he said gravely. 'It'll help them understand the theme.'

'Humph,' Ivy grunted, rolling her eyes. '*Theme.* Unless you're purchasing something, would you mind moving away from the counter, sir?'

As Amber turned an incredulous look on Ivy, Guy said smoothly, 'But I am purchasing something, Ivy. I'm buying all your stock.'

Ivy's jaw dropped. '*What?* You can't. I'll have nothing for my customers.'

'Yes, he can, Ivy,' Amber cut in firmly. She smiled at Guy. 'Maybe you could just leave us a few blooms in case we get a wild rush?'

'Aha! Do you get those too?' he said. 'I think I had one this morning, in fact.'

It was hard not to laugh with Ivy looking so dour, but Amber managed to hold it in, though she had to avoid Guy's eyes, knowing they were brimming with amusement.

Keeping his mouth grave, he pointed to the iris in her hair. 'Can you spare some of those? And we might take some of these, these, and those over there. And more of the roses. My vision of you involves lots of roses.'

Amber retrieved a delivery box from the back room, and with Serena's help started to layer in the blooms while Ivy glowered, totting up the cost like a distrustful hawk.

By the time Guy had finished selecting the flowers he wanted for his scenario they'd filled a second large box.

'What do you plan to do with them all?' Amber said when they were in the car. Divine fragrances issued from the boxes in the rear.

Guy leaned over and, cupping her face, kissed her. Along with his own exciting personal flavour, at this time of day he tasted of coffee. Although her lips still felt ten-

der from the ravages of the night, it seemed impossible to
satisfy their insatiable desire for more of him. Somehow
they would never listen to reason. Nor would her breasts
and her other erotic parts.

But, to her grateful pleasure, his exploring hands found
all her secret places through her clothes and aroused her
all over again.

Guy was similarly afflicted. 'I shouldn't have done
that,' he groaned, drawing away from her. 'You taste too
good. If the team wasn't waiting…'

Marvelling at how her eyes actually did resemble jew-
els, and at how he might even be tempted to say such a
mushy thing aloud if he didn't keep a strict check on his
tongue, Guy felt an unnerving thought flash into his head.

Not for the first time, in fact. Only now it was about to
*happen* he was seeing more clearly than ever before how
difficult it might be to keep this romance—or fling, or
whatever he was engaged in—under wraps.

If the crew cottoned on to it…

He could imagine it only too well. The trouble was they
knew too much. Most of them were aware of his ancient
history. Some had *witnessed* the event, for God's sake. He
didn't care about that any more. He was over it. He just
couldn't stand for them all to get excited. To be watching
from the sidelines, avidly appraising every move he made.
Hoping he'd be lucky this time. Whispering among themselves about whether or not he could pull it off.

Guts clenching in sudden distaste, he started the car
and reversed out of the park with an unexpected screech of
tyres. Nosing the car into the traffic stream, he said grimly,
'I'll just have to keep my hands off you today, that's all.'

Clutching her seat belt, Amber stared at him in surprise. The lines of his face seemed suddenly tense. But as

though he sensed her curiosity he relaxed his expression and flashed her a warm glance.

She glanced at the long muscled thighs appealingly encased in denim on the other side of the console. 'But I don't have to keep my hands off *you* just yet, do I?'

By the time he drove them into the basement of the steel and glass tower in Castlereagh Street, where his office was located, she'd covered a lot of territory.

After he pulled on the handbrake they each straightened their clothes. Amber checked her face in the sun visor mirror and patted her hair in place.

'What do you think? Lipstick?'

Smiling, he softly drew his forefinger across her mouth. 'No need.'

The light, sensual touch made the blood swell helplessly in her veins.

'You may be right. It'd be a crime to cover up that last kiss.'

Desire flared in his eyes and he kissed her again—another long, breathless, sexy clinch—causing them to have to go through the tidying-up procedure all over again.

He sat back then and frowned a little, squaring his shoulders. 'There is just one small point I should probably mention.'

'Yeah?' She gazed expectantly at him.

'It's about the team.' Beneath his dark brows his grey eyes were glittering with some intent calculation. 'They're a great team, but you might find—especially at first—they can seem pretty businesslike.'

She nodded. 'Well, that's good, isn't it?'

'Yeah, it's good,' he said warmly. 'It's the way it has to be. But they…er…' He gestured, evading her eyes. 'Well, they don't know about us knowing each other personally, of course.'

She studied him through her lashes. 'Well, of course. How would they?'

He flicked her a glance of amused appreciation. Then he said carefully, 'It's better they don't know.'

'Fine.' She reached and drew a finger from his cheekbone to his jaw. 'I'll try not to lust. And I promise I won't blab about what you were doing at three o'clock this morning.'

He gave a small laugh. 'I know you won't do that. But because they won't understand the real situation, I just don't want you to feel as if anyone's trying to—push you around.'

'Why would I feel like that?'

He waggled his hand. 'Well, they can be a little abrupt. I know how sensitive you are, and I'd hate you to take it personally. They're used to dealing with professional models. So if anyone gives you instructions, or comments on your appearance, you need to understand it will be strictly for professional purposes.'

'I see.' She nodded.

'The thing is…' He hesitated. 'I would hate your tender feelings to be hurt.'

She thought of some of the savage insults the director of the ballet company had been likely to shriek at the dancers when rehearsal wasn't going well. It was tempting to laugh, but his concern was so genuine, so kind, she was filled with a fierce tenderness for him. She just squeezed his knee and gave him a reassuring grin.

'Relax. I'm used to showbiz. Don't you know I'm an O'Neill?'

'Oh, I know.' His eyes gleamed.

Still, she wondered if she was imagining he looked a bit stressed.

Up on the forty-eighth floor a small group was waiting

to meet her. There was an older guy, one young executive type in his late twenties, a youngish red-haired boy, and two capable-looking women—one with flaming hair who introduced herself as Maggie.

As Guy had predicted, they all shook hands with Amber in a friendly and professional manner, then promptly forgot she was human.

A wall screen glowed with a picture of a beautiful fifteenth century painting of people in a garden wearing long floaty dresses. Amber wasn't sure which one of the characters was supposed to represent her, because no one bothered to explain. She tilted her head to read the label printed along the side of the reproduction. *La Primavera* it was called. Spring.

They strolled around her, discussing her attributes as a model so frankly Amber was glad she'd been warned. Still, it was all quite clinical. She might as well have been a blow-up doll.

Guy stood by while they inspected her from top to toe, not commenting much, but clearly in command. Since the car park he'd morphed into 'The Boss'. She had to keep looking at him to believe he was the same person who'd borrowed her toothbrush, then actually confessed.

His demeanour made it clear to any interested parties that though he might have seen her flower shop in the distance *once*, by pure chance only, she remained a total stranger to him. Lucky she was no stranger to the way professionals worked behind the scenes, or she might have been offended.

The team directed comments to Guy from time to time, but his replies were minimal, as if he didn't want to join the party. Amber noticed they kept sending him faintly surprised looks.

His eyes were inscrutable, but alert, and there was a

certain tension in his posture as they pulled her apart.
Nothing about her was sacred, it seemed. Her face, her fig-
ure, her hands, legs and ankles. Even her knees. All came
under discussion and, though most bits seemed to pass the
photobility test, she flinched at some of the comments.

'If she was even an inch taller…'

*Ha.* They had to be *kidding.* She'd been one of the tall-
est in the company. What did they want? A giraffe?

Guy seemed to feel the same way. 'How tall do you
want her, André?' he said pleasantly. 'That height looks
excellent to me.'

'Oh sure, sure. I was only thinking of, you know, screen
presence.'

'Doesn't beauty count for anything?' Guy said mildly.
'Grace?'

He flushed a little after he'd said that, and Amber felt
herself pinken. There was a small silence. People were ex-
changing astounded glances with each other, then someone hastened to say, 'Oh, yeah—sure, boss.'

Amber made a face at Guy but he pretended not to
catch it. After a fraught second the torture started again.

'Turn this way, dear. No, the other way. The right is
her best.'

'Look up there, sweetheart. Now walk over to the desk.
Now back.'

'Oh, yes, yes. Lovely walk. Look at those calves. And
the arms. Nice muscle tone.'

They didn't mention her behind, though she felt pretty
certain Guy was holding his breath waiting for it.

One of the women's jobs was to write instructions onto
a notepad as fast as they fell from the experts' lips.

'That's it, that's it!' someone exclaimed. 'If we can
catch her like *that.* Watch for that angle, André.'

'What about her hair?' the older guy asked. 'Do you want it up or—?'

'Down,' Guy cut in. 'Definitely.'

'Shouldn't we turn her into a blonde?'

'Why?' Guy said sharply. 'Her hair's a rainbow. Catch her in the sun and you'll see it's filled with light. It's rich in chestnut, reds, golds, violets.'

He checked himself, blinking a couple of times. Amber thought she could detect another faint stain to his cheek.

'Anyway, there's no time,' he added curtly, deflecting more startled glances from his team.

'Yeah, course. Fine,' the older man hastened to reply. 'Works for me.' He shrugged and sent Amber a wink.

'What about that costume? I could have put something really good together if I'd had more advance notice,' Maggie grumbled in an aside. 'What's the big rush, anyway?'

There was a small silence while people held their breaths.

'Are you saying you can't do it, Maggie?' When he spoke Guy's tone was level. Pleasant, even. But it left an edge that had Maggie scrambling to backtrack.

'Oh, heavens—course not. I have one or two things we can use. I'll just have to do a few tweaks here and there.' The sudden tension in the room relaxed as Maggie got herself off the hook.

'Which one is it?' Amber enquired.

'Here.' Guy directed her gaze to a lady in the picture wearing a delicate floral gown, her hair decked in flowers. She was scattering roses from some she carried in the apron of her skirt.

'We need to put you in a floaty number like one of these.'

Amber stared at the screen. With the lighting behind it

the picture looked almost transparent. 'Floaty?' she murmured doubtfully. 'It's not see-through, is it?'

'Yeah, see-through.' The young red-haired guy guffawed, nudging his neighbour and grinning. 'Exactly.'

Guy turned a stern glance on the boy, then coolly beckoned him aside. The lad's grin was wiped. Whatever Guy had murmured to him was inaudible to everyone else, but the boy visibly wilted. When he slunk back to rejoin the team he didn't look nearly so chipper.

Amber felt so sorry for him. It was soul-destroying to be shamed in front of a group. Honestly, Guy needed to get a grip. To make matters worse, he intercepted the sympathetic glance she gave the boy and sent her a warning frown.

What the…! He wasn't deluded into thinking he was *her* boss now, was he?

Amber noticed Maggie shooting glances between her and Guy, and had the sinking feeling the game was up.

'All right—er—Amber,' Guy said briskly, suddenly seeming to pull himself together. 'Maggie'll take you down now for some make-up.' He turned his gaze in Amber's direction. But only in her direction, not right *to* her. He didn't meet her eyes, as a friend would. Or an acquaintance from the local flower shop. Even a perfect stranger who'd just happened in off the street.

Only lovers covering up tried not to gaze at each other. She knew it, Maggie knew it, and she wouldn't have been surprised if the whole crew knew it.

She'd have laughed if Guy hadn't been so concerned about his team knowing. At the same time she felt her insides melting with love for him for not being able to conceal his passion.

Maggie's manner as she beckoned Amber to follow her made Amber wonder if the woman was peeved about something. She hustled her along to a suite of wardrobe rooms not unlike the rooms backstage at a theatre, though on a much smaller scale. Then after measuring her, without much ceremony Maggie pushed, prodded and pinned her into a variety of dresses.

Usually Amber adored the whole costume business, and entered into the spirit of the thing with gusto. This time the experience was bit too brusque to enjoy.

'This feels quite tight,' she suggested to Maggie as she was being pinned into a long dress.

'Hmm.' Standing with pins in her mouth, a stapler in her hand and a tape around her neck, Maggie was the picture of the long-suffering seamstress. 'Hang on while I clamp this bodice.'

'*Oof.* I do have to breathe, you know.'

'Think how it enhances your shape. He'll love it.' Maggie glanced at her then, a challenge in her eyes.

Amber didn't waste time pretending not to know who Maggie meant. She just lifted her brows haughtily. 'So long as it works for his scenario, Maggie. That's all Guy will be interested in.'

Maggie glowered, focused on her pinning. After a while she said fiercely, 'Guy's a *nice man*. He's not the sort who plays around with people.'

It was Amber's turn to frown. Did this Maggie assume *she* was the sort to play around with people? She was strongly tempted to inform Maggie that she actually found Guy really very playful, but decided against it. She and Guy were none of the woman's business.

Besides, she didn't want to risk being stuck with pins.

Once she was back in her own clothes again, a young woman introduced as Kate sat her in front of a fluoro lit mirror and started smoothing stuff onto her face.

Maggie's phone buzzed and she turned away to deal

with it. 'Thanks, boss.' Slipping the phone away, she turned to Amber and Kate. 'Guy's given us an hour. Where's that picture?'

There was a massive amount of hustle, with Maggie darting about collecting things in between madly machining darts into the dress to make it fit. Meanwhile, Kate worked magic on Amber's face and powdered her throat

When her make-up was done to their satisfaction, Maggie helped her back into the dress. It was ivory, with a deep-scooped neckline, long lacy sleeves and a softly billowing skirt.

'I'm not sure,' Amber said doubtfully, trying to suck in her tummy while Maggie fastened at least a hundred buttons. 'The fabric's good, but I don't know how spring-like it is. It feels a bit as if I should be walking up the aisle of Westminster Abbey.' She surveyed Maggie's copy of the picture again. 'Do you really think this dress will cut it?'

'It'll just have to do,' Maggie said grimly, piling flowers onto her workbench. 'It's long, isn't it? If people don't give you any notice to work miracles they have to be satisfied with what they get. Italian paintings, for pity's sake. What next? Did the boys bring up that other box of flowers, Kate?' She started rooting through shelves of plastic packing boxes. 'Don't you worry, my love. We'll tart you up with so many flowers old Botticelli himself wouldn't know the difference.'

Guy stood staring through his precious viewfinder at the Chinese Garden of Friendship. His camera team—André and the red-haired boy—lounged on the grass. As an informal make-up station for Kate, they'd set up a folding table and a couple of chairs.

The location looked tranquil enough, with its waterfalls, willow lawns and charming little bridges. At least this time early on a Tuesday afternoon every man and his dog were partying somewhere else. Apart from the risk of accidentally including a pagoda in the shot, there had to be at least one good angle here where a goddess could scatter roses.

Guy decided on the most likely spot and galvanised the red-haired boy to help him distribute a few of Amber's flowers about. 'Try to make it look natural,' he said, stapling a rose to a twig. 'Remember she's a flower goddess.'

The boy started to speak, then checked himself, casting Guy an anxious look to see if he'd heard. Guy made a wry grimace to himself. He'd seen their knowing glances. He knew they were surmising over his relationship with Amber.

He gritted his teeth. Why couldn't they all get over it and let him get on with his life? It seemed that everyone he knew was constantly on the lookout for a happy ending for him. Of the *marriage* variety. As if that was the only kind of ending that counted.

If only people understood how humiliating that was.

Normally he loved a shoot. This was what he enjoyed most: seeing his vision come to life and capturing it on camera. It was a beautiful day, the city traffic was barely audible here, and he was about to see Amber looking even more impossibly desirable than ever.

He had to admit, though, he was having second thoughts. Not about Amber. Hell, no. Just thinking of her made his heart beat faster. *And* the sex. How had he survived so long in the wilderness without a warm, lovely body to curl up to?

No, it was *this* that was wrong. Involving his team in his personal affairs. Risking dragging it all up again. How could he have forgotten that some of them were friends with Jo? The other day Maggie had even casually dropped in to the conversation that Jo was back in Sydney. As if *he* might be interested.

For pity's sake.

But what if one of them hinted something to Amber? She'd be racing for the nearest set of hills like a horrified gazelle. Embarrassed.

Even worse, she'd be embarrassed for *him*. Imagining her reaction, he felt himself start to sweat. He ran a finger around the inside of his shirt collar. If only there was some way he could insulate her from people who knew him.

It had definitely been a mistake, rushing to her rescue like that. Who did he think he was? Sir Galahad?

But was it too late to call a halt today? He was nearly as good with a camera as André. If he could come up with a reasonable excuse he could send them all off home and do the whole shoot himself.

He was just racking his brains for one when the sound of voices echoing down the path alerted him to the approach of the women.

His pulse quickened. His vision was about to crystallise. Enter Spring.

Kate appeared first, carrying a box with her make-up case balanced on top, while Maggie walked alongside Amber, holding her bunched up skirt off the ground. At first glance the three were all clumped together. It took Guy's bedazzled brain a moment to separate them into their individual components.

The same instant he did, Maggie allowed the dress she was holding to fall around Amber, and stepped away from her. Guy's lungs seized as something like a twelve bore shotgun blasted a hole through him.

What were they thinking? They'd done her up as a bride.

The women fluttered around her, tweaking her dress

and the little flower sprays pinned all over her—at her bosom, her waist, on her skirt. A wreath of pink, red and white flowers adorned her head, while more were plaited through her long hair.

André and the lad hauled themselves up off the grass and clustered around her, goggling as if they'd never seen a woman with a pretty cleavage before in their lives.

The boy kept saying, 'You look hot, Amber. Hot.'

'Nice one, Maggie.' That was André, circling Amber like a grinning shark.

'Thanks, boys,' Maggie said. 'Scrubbed up all right, didn't she?'

Guy saw Amber give them a quick modest smile, then look straight to him for his reaction. Thing was, he couldn't say anything right then. A cold wind was whistling through the space in his guts.

He read puzzlement in her blue eyes, and had to turn away before he disgraced himself with some blistering comment.

André swanned into the foreground, salivating like Mr Fox. 'Stand over here, Amber, and let me see you with the trees behind you.' Smooth as butter, kneeling down with the camera on his shoulder, pretending he was interested in the shot when it was plain to anyone with half a brain he just wanted an excuse to ogle her.

The boy just continued gaping with his mouth open.

With superhuman resolve Guy snapped himself together. This was his disaster. He was in charge and he'd set the course.

Blinking, he said, 'Let's not waste time oohing and aahing. Thanks, Maggie, that'll have to do, though I'm not sure a wedding was quite what I had in mind. Did you bring some roses for her to scatter?'

They were all looking strangely at him. Maggie's hand

flew to her mouth in a betraying little gesture of dismayed comprehension that jabbed his raw spot like a knife.

And Amber…

What had he done? The hurt in her face, the confusion. How harsh had he sounded? What had he actually *said*? He closed his eyes, trying to recall his exact words, his blood pressure pounding in his temples.

What was wrong with him? She wasn't a bride. This was another time, another place, and he was two years older. Amber O'Neill *was not a bride*.

'Amber,' he said hoarsely, shielding his eyes against the sun so as not to see his vision too clearly, 'show us how you can walk like the springtime.'

# CHAPTER TEN

THE shoot took longer than Amber had anticipated. She was asked to float like a goddess and scatter roses so many times their store ran out. Then people had to scramble about picking them up again.

Guy seemed a little worried about how she was standing up to the repetition, but after a while he relaxed. If she'd wanted to she could have reminded him she was used to far more strenuous exertion at a highly concentrated level. But she didn't care to bring up her past glories. Not in front of the crew.

Eventually the strained atmosphere mellowed slightly, thank goodness, and there were even some fun moments when the whole company collapsed in laughter, though it was an edgy sort of laughter. Guy joined in, but something in him felt different. Not so much a coolness, as a quietness.

A reserve.

When he and André were finally satisfied with their footage, and they'd wrapped up, the crew congratulated Amber and told her she'd been excellent. Professional, André said. Maggie especially seemed to be making an effort to be kind, actually suggesting she might drop by the shop the next time she was in Kirribilli. Amber was scratching her head. Had Maggie forgotten her dastardly plan to run off with her beloved boss and screw his brains out?

She noticed Guy look too hard at Maggie when she made that astounding suggestion. The lines around his mouth were rather grim.

The trip home had a vastly different mood from the morning's. Guy didn't have much to say, while Amber felt anxious and confused. Awash with misgivings, in truth. Considering how frankly passionate he'd been towards her a few hours ago, this constraint was depressing. The big question was *why*? What had she done to make him go off her so dramatically?

'Do you think the shoot went well?' she ventured at last, her heart thumping like an idiot's.

He nodded. 'Oh, yeah. I'm pretty sure we'll be able to do something with it.'

She made her tone bright and upbeat. 'What a relief. What happens next?'

'Well, we'll edit it. Play around with it to get the tones and colours right. Layer on some music, of course. Something to suit the motion of the piece. A voiceover, some graphics…' He smiled to himself. Or maybe it was a grimace of nauseated derision.

'Plenty of airbrushing, I hope?'

He shrugged. 'Maybe a bit of enhancement. To the dress,' he finished, with a rather sibilant hiss.

She was silent for a while, wondering if she'd imagined that he was burning with resentment over something. 'Sounds like a lot of work.'

'Yep. The next part will have to be filmed in your shop.'

'Oh?' She glanced at him in surprise. 'You mean there's more?'

'Only a couple of seconds' worth. But that couple of seconds will have to show the shop in the best light possible. I'm thinking we may as well send the people who do our set designs around to start your makeover.'

She felt a flutter of excitement followed by anxiety about how much it must all be costing.

She glanced at him, hesitating. 'Look, I'm so grateful to you for all this, Guy. Honestly. Offering all your resources, your—your people. It's so very generous. Truly kind. But I can't help worrying about the money. I know it must be costing you heaps.'

He frowned, embarrassed, and shook his head. 'No need to feel like that. This is business. If we can make Fleur Elise attractive, the glow will reflect on Wilder Solutions. When you're rich we'll add it to the bill.'

'No,' she said firmly, a decision she'd been mulling over for weeks suddenly crystallising in her mind. 'That's good of you, but—I want to pay for my own renovations. It'll be great if you recommend your designer. But I'll pay for all the work and the materials myself.'

He looked sharply at her, but didn't question her ability to pay. Just as well. She had no intention of asking anyone's permission to seek a small business loan from her bank. It was her shop, and it was her decision. She'd borrow the bare minimum and use some of the money for stock.

He glanced at her, his grey eyes appraising. 'Would you object if I suggested a couple of guys that could do the actual work?'

'No, of course not. So long as they're excellent.' Amber smiled, pleased with her decision. She glanced at him. 'Will I be wearing the same costume for the shop part of the ad?'

He drew in a sharp breath through his nostrils. *'No.'*

Amber started. The harsh syllable echoed in her ears as the air crackled with tension.

What was wrong with him? So he hated that dress. Or was it her? Questions kept popping into her head, only for her to dismiss them just as quickly. Whatever was eating him had to do with her *in* the dress, obviously. She herself hadn't thought it a great representation of the gown in the painting. Was he still mad because Maggie had failed to realise his divine vision?

Something had happened today. And she had the feeling the crew—or at least some of them—were in on it. She'd noticed the hurried exchange of glances and Maggie's unhappy face.

As they approached the Harbour Bridge, against all her prudent instincts she asked tentatively, 'Have you worked with Maggie a long time?'

'Yep.'

'She seems to think a lot of you.'

He glanced searchingly at her, eyes narrowed, a sudden tension in his manner. 'Yeah? What did she tell you?'

'Nothing—except that you're a wonderful guy.'

'Now, why would Maggie feel compelled to say that?' The words sounded casual. But there was an edge she didn't miss.

She shrugged guiltily. Maggie had talked about him, and now *she* had foolishly blabbed. She tried to get out of it by being flippant. 'How do I know? She could just be a compulsive liar. Or maybe she has a secret crush on you.'

The man was not amused. She could tell. Partly by his heavy beetling brows. Partly by the hardening of his jaw for the several blocks between the bridge and home.

Maybe she should just shut up if everything she said was wrong. But she couldn't bear it when people were mad at her and she didn't even know what she'd done. Maybe he was regretting his generous impulse and getting stuck with having to make this ad for her. Or perhaps he resented her invading his workplace, getting to know his team.

Or maybe... Her heart turned to ice. The taboo thought that had been lurking all day suddenly materialised.

Just *maybe* it was over.

The signs were all there. Call her a spineless coward, but while this was the ideal opportunity to clear it up, she dreaded knowing.

For the remainder of the trip she vacillated between asking and not asking. If she did, it would be a terrible risk. It might make him feel pressured. In her experience, put a man under pressure and you'd most likely face a rejection. But Guy seemed to be on the brink of rejecting her anyway. If she had any self-respect she should at least toughen up and find out why. She owed herself that much, didn't she?

By the time they drew up into his parking spot in the arcade basement her insides were quaking and she had that strangulated feeling in her chest.

There was a tense moment when neither of them spoke.

She was the one who broke the silence, gazing straight ahead to keep her voice steady. 'I was just wondering why you weren't very pleased with me in the scene? Why you looked at me as if you wanted to throw up? As if you— couldn't stand the sight of me.' She tried to sound super-cool and in control, but towards the end her chin insisted on wobbling, and that came through in her voice.

His hands flexed on the wheel. 'No, Amber.' He ground out the words. 'That's *not*—true. Not—how it was.'

There was a remorseful intensity in his voice that might have meant he was being truthful, or might have meant he was riddled with guilt. Guilty as sin for wanting to dump her on the nearest rubbish tip.

He turned to her, his eyes ablaze with some unreadable emotion. 'I know I may have seemed a bit taken aback when I first— But that had nothing to do with you. Honestly.'

'Didn't it?' After all she'd endured today, this was just too much. Her veins swelled with indignation. 'Well, I've got news for you, Guy Wilder. It feels pretty personal when someone glares at you as if you look like a slug.'

He made a jerky gesture. 'I'm sorry, sweetheart. Honestly. It wasn't *you*.'

At least he wasn't trying to deny the ghastly moment had happened.

'Who was it, then?'

He grew silent, his face hardening to a cool, unreadable mask. Then he lifted his shoulders. 'Look, we all have *things* in our lives we don't want to talk about. When I saw you at that moment just for an instant I was reminded of something that happened once. A long time ago...' He waved his hands. '*Ages* ago now. It was just one of those stupid flashbacks from out of the blue. It was nothing, I swear. It's all ancient history, but just for a minute there it hit me. All right?'

She stared down at her hands, mulling over all the denials, all the minimalising, then flicked him a glance. 'Was it her? That woman you were with before? The one you had a break-up with?'

He closed his eyes and sighed. 'Look, Amber, let's just leave it now. Shall we?'

'Fine.' Shrugging, she released the seat belt and got out of the car.

It was blindingly apparent now why he was over her. Today she'd reminded him of someone else. The woman he wished he was still with.

When they each stood outside their respective doors, he drew in a breath and glanced at her, as if he was bracing himself to say something difficult. Something like, *Well, it's been fun. But I think you understand it can't ever be anything more than that. I've just realised I still have this deep-seated passion for my old love. So…sorry Amber. No more hanging out. See ya round.*

But Amber got in first.

She glanced in his direction and yawned. 'Well, it's been a big day. I hope I can stay awake long enough to finish my management assignment tonight.'

His brow creased. 'Oh? So you'll be staying in for dinner?'

She avoided his eyes. 'I'm not that hungry. I'll probably just make a sandwich.'

He flicked a glance at her, then frowned at the floor. 'Right.'

'So…' She unlocked her door, hesitated. 'See you, then.'

She could feel his grey gaze sear her face like a torch. But then he just gave up. Just like that. The guy who was worried he'd ruined all his chances with her.

'Okay,' he said. 'Good luck with it. See you.'

Inside, she bumped her shin on the edge of the coffee table in the hall. Cursing in extreme agony, it occurred to her that she'd rather have this pain than the one she knew was about to slice up her heart once the full ramifications sank through.

Whatever Guy *said*, however much he declared that woman was in his past, he was still in love with her. Why else would he have been so affected today?

In fact, now she'd been shown a glimpse of the bigger picture, a few thousand little clues began to add up.

She limped into the kitchen and opened the fridge, smarting all over. He hadn't been concerned about not having dinner with her. There hadn't been the least sign of disappointment. Since when had a management assign-

ment taken precedence over a night of excitement and romance?

Simple. Since the romance had hit a rock.

As she stared gloomily into the freezer, an even more
lowering thought struck.

It was clear she must resemble that woman pretty
closely. That must be why he'd been attracted to her. It
had never been anything to do with her personally at all.

Tears swam into her eyes. All the time he'd been making love to Amber O'Neill, cuddling her, saying all those
passionate things, he'd really been thinking of his true
love. He was probably thinking of her right now.

Searching for a silver lining while she was choking
down her toasted cheese sandwich, it did occur to her that
he hadn't actually said goodbye yet. Maybe she should
have tried to seduce him good and proper to drive that
woman from his mind? But not in the car. Not in a car
park. There could be nothing 'grand passion' about that
sort of venue.

Anyway, he'd looked too remote. If only he'd said something warm. Something to give her hope.

It was all too distressing. Instinct told her there'd be
no accidental meeting tonight. How was she to kill time?
She supposed she could shift all the furniture back into
the sitting room and watch TV. Though that would require
energy and motivation, when she urgently needed distrac-
tion. If she was to get through the next few hours she *had*
to have something to paralyse her brain. Even her assignment was starting to look like an option.

With a groan of surrender she got up and switched on
her notebook. Sighing, she clicked open the file. The pre-
reading she'd already done had been about as exciting as
the arcade on a Sunday afternoon. *'Supervision of staff '*,

she read. Yeah, fat chance anyone had ever had of super-
vising *her* staff.

She read on and, surprisingly, started to become quite
absorbed. At some point she must have stopped listening
for sounds from next door, for clues of Guy's activities, because before she knew it she was in the zone, writing some
pretty hard-hitting stuff about Ivy. Not mentioning her by
name, of course. But if ever there was a bona fide case
study requiring a management plan Ivy was the candidate.

Maybe because she was miserable and confused, she
found the plan was a great outlet. In a way it was like cho-
reography, and she'd always found that satisfying. She'd
just finished designing some seriously rugged hoops for
Ivy to hop through when she noticed the time was close
on eleven.

She rubbed her eyes, then gave the great work one last
read through before hitting the 'save' button. Rising and
stretching, she headed for her bedroom. At least she'd
achieved something today.

Like a lorryload of boulders, her memory and the
day's events crashed into her heart. There'd be nothing
else for Amber O'Neill tonight but an empty bed and a
good night's sleep.

Grabbing a fresh nightie, she headed for the bathroom.


Guy frowned over his text. How to encourage customers to think Fleur Elise first when they desired their little
piece of spring? It was tempting to write a whole bunch of
poetic lyrics, but the film-maker in him knew that in this
case less was better. Nothing could be as powerful as the
image of Amber floating through that garden.

His heart quickened. She was as lovely as the roses
they'd decked her in.

Oh, for God's sake, why couldn't he have controlled

himself? He leapt up and started to pace his aunt's sitting room. What a fool he'd been. The very thing he needed to bury, once and for all, was now back in the headlines with his film crew. The whole office was probably abuzz by now. Speculating about his 'new relationship'.

He shuddered. How he hated those words. Useless to hope Amber never found out about his laughable history. If Maggie didn't tell her, someone else would.

With cold misgiving he contemplated the future. He could see it clearly now. The longer Amber stayed with him, the more likely it was she'd be meeting his friends. Already he'd planned to talk a couple of the Blue Suede boys into giving her a hand with her shop.

And wasn't the Suede's big night coming up? He slapped his forehead. He'd been so obsessed with her he'd neglected to think ahead. She'd be meeting the guys *and* their girlfriends. Not to mention everyone at The Owl who'd remember him and Jo from the old days.

Someone would be eager to fill her in. He could just imagine how the sordid tale might be presented. No doubt with a whole lot of schmaltzy spin about how he'd been destroyed forever—shattered, et cetera.

As if he was some sort of lily-livered comedian. He punched his fist into his palm. It flashed through his head that he might just have to grit his teeth and tell her himself first. Some of it, anyway.

If he could just work out what to say in advance. Maybe there was a way to keep it low-key. If he could think of it as a script. A technical challenge…

Amber lay back in the chamomile-scented water and closed her eyes. In the grim reality of not having heard from Guy for hours the chopped-up feeling in her chest had intensified. There'd been nothing. Not even a text. It was crushing to think of how empty her life would be if he dropped her. There'd be nothing to look forward to.

But what if they continued to see each other? Being besotted was one thing. It was all about having fun with someone. But where was the fun now? Somewhere along the way she'd gone much further than that.

She had to face it. She was madly in love with him. Oh, she'd known it for ages, but never so strikingly as in the car this evening. Even if he still wanted to play with her, could she go on with him knowing she was a mere substitute?

She was roused from her dismal reflections by a sharp ring of her doorbell. *Hah!*

She sat upright. It could only be him at this hour. With a surge of fearful excitement she heaved herself out of the tub, gave herself a hasty towelling, then dragged on her silk wrap.

At the front door she stood hesitating, momentarily paralysed with fear about what he might be going to say. She switched on the hall light. 'Who is it?'

There was a loaded pause. Then Guy's voice came, deep and subdued. 'It's me.'

She opened the door. He was standing with head lowered, though he glanced up at once. His eyes sparked when he saw her state of undress, but his expression was serious.

Her heart started to thump. Was this *it*? He'd come to make the cut? He had on the black tee shirt that so enhanced his gorgeous arms and made him look dangerously handsome. As well, her eagle eye noticed he'd shaved. Had he been out? Or was there some other reason he needed a smooth jaw at eleven-thirty at night?

'Hi,' he said, his deep voice sonorous. 'I was thinking it might be good to talk.'

'Oh? Well, I—I was just bathing.'

His eyes assessed her with that piercing gleam. 'You smell fresh. Sorry if I interrupted. Tub or shower?'

'Tub.' He was no stranger to her tub. She pulled the edges of her wrap closer, moistened her lips. 'Come through.'

She led the way to the kitchen. Quite a few of their most exciting evenings had started in her kitchen. She could tell by the light in his eyes he was aware of that too. Even so, there was a purpose in his demeanour that didn't suggest seduction.

They faced each other standing, like adversaries, and she noticed his brows edge together as he considered his words. He drew in a breath. 'Er…about what we talked about…'

'The ad?'

His eyes narrowed in rebuke of her little tease. 'No, not the *ad*. The…the thing I—I remembered today. The… er…the flashback.'

'Oh, the woman, you mean?'

He lifted an impatient shoulder, then opened his hands. 'Look, you knew I wasn't a virgin. It's pretty hard to reach thirty-three without having a few re— *lovers* along the way.'

'Of course. Not that it's any of my business. We aren't exactly a couple.' She gave a silvery little laugh at the very absurdity of the idea.

His face smoothed. Some of the tension leaked from his posture. 'Exactly. So, if I went out with a woman a few times, naturally certain circumstances could bring her to mind. Or any other woman I might have dated. I don't know why you thought it was such a big thing.' He lowered his lashes. 'No doubt you've kissed a guy before.'

She delivered her sweetest smile. 'Though rarely ever so well. What's her name?'

He blinked and turned his eyes away. 'Look, what difference—?' He threw out his hands in exasperation. 'All
right. It's Jo. All right?'

Amber couldn't speak for a second. She could easily
loathe, despise and ridicule a woman from the past if a
mere fleeting memory of her was capable of paralysing
her lover for hours. But once that woman had a *name*…

And a nice name. The sort of name one of her girlfriends might have had.

'She must have been quite special to you?'

He looked non-committal. Shrugged. 'For a while.
Yeah, she was. But these things end, don't they? It's no
big deal.'

She gazed steadily at him. He must have quickly re-
viewed his last words, because he hastened to correct any
poor impression they might have left.

'Look, I liked her for a while. Okay? But I'm glad I'm
not with her any more.'

She nodded, relieved he'd said that even if she wasn't
sure how true it was. 'I see.'

'Do you, though?' He looked keenly at her. 'I like *you*,
Amber. I *really* like you.' His eyes were intent on her face,
ablaze with sincerity.

'Oh.' She flushed, her ridiculous heart rushing and fluttering like a trapped insect. 'Well, I like you too, Guy.'

His expression lightened. Smiling, he pulled her towards him. 'Even after I was so prickly with you today?'
He started to nuzzle her hair, face and throat with his lips.

'Yeah. And you *were*, you know. It made me think I
must look just like her.'

*'No.'* He took her shoulders and gazed into her eyes,
denial in every line of his face. 'You don't,' he said with
conviction. 'Not at all. Not in the slightest. You look like
your own unique and beautiful self.'

He pulled her close to him again, holding her and stroking her as though she genuinely was someone rare and precious. She could feel his big heart thudding against her own.

Call her an obsessive, but curiosity needed to be appeased. 'What does she look like?'

He gave a sigh of exasperation. 'It doesn't *matter* what she looks like. I never want to lay eyes on her again.'

'I'm glad.' She kissed his Adam's apple. 'What colour's her hair?'

*'Amber.'* He grabbed her shoulders and gazed sternly at her. 'What difference does it make? I'm telling you... Look, the last time I saw her she had short reddish hair. Okay?'

'Fine. It makes no earthly difference to *me*. Not a bit. I just like to have a mental picture, that's all. You're the vision man. You must know what that's like.'

He sighed. 'What else can I say to you?' His lips moved against her ear. 'She's short and stocky with freckles. And you know what I'm thinking now?'

'What?' She held her breath in sudden hopeful anticipation.

'It's high time I took a bath.' Desire deepened his voice.

'Oh.' She smiled, partly in self-mockery at her weakness. 'You poor man. You're too late. Sadly the water will now be cold.'

He grinned, his usual cocksure confidence reasserting itself. 'I think you know I can heat it up.'

In truth, the bath was one of his better inspirations. It eased away the doubts and pains of the day. There was much playful loving, and even more serious, panting loving. One thing about being in a bath was the total nakedness it imposed. There was no possibility of lying or deceiving someone when you were both stripped bare and washed by the same water.

In the new, though still careful spirit of sharing, she confessed a little about the Miguel fiasco, and the swathe he'd cut through her friends in the ballet company. She only related the barest minimum, of course, sensing it wouldn't be wise for Guy to focus on her former relationship, however scant it had been.

She sighed. 'I think the worst thing…this probably sounds vain and pathetic…but I honestly think the worst thing was how much of a fool I felt. How absolutely *diminished* in the eyes of my friends. Can you understand that?'

He pulled her closer to him. 'Oh, I can.' There was heartfelt conviction in his tone. Then he said fiercely, 'What was *wrong* with the guy? What the hell else would he want in a woman?'

At that she broke into laughter. 'Variety?'

And he was so understanding, so warmly comforting, at the same time as making her laugh at some of the things that had so mortified her, she felt her intimate confession draw her closer to him. As if by sharing that tiny snippet of her historical truth they'd passed through a door.

His arms were still around her, hers around him, their hearts beating as one, when she said, 'What happened with Jo that made you end it?'

She felt him go quite still. Then he said matter-of-factly, 'Oh, she ended it.'

She stayed still herself, listening to her heart thundering in the gathering silence. Then she said, 'What did she say?'

'Nothing. She stood me up. '

'On a date?'

He made a sardonic face. 'Yes. A date.'

'So you just…?' She stared at him in surprise. 'What? No second chances?'

It took him a while to reply, and when he did it was brief. 'Nope.'

# CHAPTER ELEVEN

IVY didn't take kindly to jumping through hoops.

She refused to say cheery things to customers, either to compliment them on their choices or wish them a beautiful day. And when the interior designer dropped in to discuss with Amber and the staff the kind of renovations they dreamed, of Ivy wanted no part of the wasteful business. Instead she hovered, glowering, among the ferns.

Even so, their discussions were fruitful. Serena, with her artistic flair, came up with some fantastic ideas that were in tune with Amber's. The designer took on board everything they said and made several of her own suggestions about fittings, wallpapers and shelving, showing Amber online site after online site where she could view the amazing array of choices.

Inspired by Guy's theme for the advertising campaign, after much mulling and discussion, Amber had come to a decision. She understood some of her management difficulties stemmed from her need to break with the past and stamp her own personality on the business.

Since Fleur Elise had been her mother's name for the shop, Amber decided to rename it with something more significant to herself. When she told the designer her idea of calling the shop La Primavera, after the old painting Guy had used for her ad, the designer's eyes lit up. She

went away to work on a 'spring' design, then e-mailed
Amber some sketches.

Amber was thrilled with them. Suddenly everything
seemed possible.

In the shop, that was. On the ninth floor, nothing could
be taken for granted. For one thing, Jean and Stuart would
be back home in a few days, and Guy would be moving
back into his house in Woollahra. It wasn't so far from
Kirribilli, as the crow flew, but since it was on the other
side of the harbour Amber knew it would feel like a million miles.

How long would he keep seeing her? It would hardly be
every night. Their accidental meetings would have to end.
If they were to continue with any sort of meaning, some
more binding form of acknowledgement of their relationship would be required. She didn't even have the status of
girlfriend. So what was she? A fling?

And since the night of the bath, though Guy had treated
her with more tenderness than ever, something was on
his mind. He was forever frowning to himself, failing to
hear things she said to him. Sometimes he studied her
when he thought she wasn't looking, searching her face
as if answers to the mysteries of the pyramids might be
encoded there.

It made her anxious and unsettled and prone to gloomy
imaginings—most of them starting with J.

'Is something on your mind?' She made this tentative
enquiry when Guy was driving her to The Owl for a pub
night.

Imagine *her*, Amber O'Neill, en route to a *pub night*.
Strangely, though, she was keen to go and had dressed ac-
cordingly, applying loads of smudgy eyeliner and shadow
that gave her a sultry siren ambience. She had the feeling

Guy wasn't exactly comfortable with it. There was an aura of tension percolating around him.

'Are you worrying about how your band will do?'

She could understand if he was. The Owl was a popular venue for bands starting up, he'd explained. He'd been so enthusiastic at first when his friends, the Blue Suede, had been offered a performance slot. Since then, though, he seemed to have cooled off.

Having heard the Suede in rehearsal, Amber could appreciate his doubts.

Feeling the weight of her clear blue gaze, Guy hastened to allay her suspicions.

'More the song,' he lied, giving himself a mental slap for betraying his—whatever. Edginess? Cool was what was needed tonight. If he was to be on display to a bunch of old acquaintances whose most recent memory of him was…

He started to sweat. No. He wouldn't think of it. He'd stare them all down and act as if it had never happened.

If he could just get through this one night, the next time and the times after should be a cinch. With grim amusement he reflected that if he survived long enough he might eventually live the whole sorry saga down.

So long as he could trust old friends to act like friends. Trouble was, it was such an entertaining story. There was bound to be some mischievous soul who felt compelled to fill Amber in.

Amber noticed his knuckles whiten on the wheel. Her trouble sensors pricked up their ears. Something was up.

She said carefully, 'You know, I've had the feeling you aren't all that keen for me to come.'

She heard him draw breath, the tiny beat as he sought the right words, and with a pang her misgivings deepened. Was *she* the problem?

'Not at all,' he said smoothly. 'I'm just wondering how much you'll enjoy it.' He cast her a teasing look. 'You know there'll be an awful noise?'

'Huh! The cheek of that.'

He flashed her a smile. 'You think you're up to it?'

She narrowed her eyes at him in disbelief. She'd only made Serena transfer a whole flock of butterflies up her arm, starting from the inside of her wrist. 'Let me get this straight. Are you saying I'm a nerd?'

He laughed. 'Hell, no.'

'I have *been* to a pub, you know. I have drunk beer.'

'You don't say?'

But though he grinned her doubts deepened. She felt mystified. He couldn't *really* be worried about how she'd react to a few bands? If it was about her, it wasn't *that*. Anyway, now the challenge had been issued. Even if a night of boy bands was worse than a week in prison, she'd enjoy it if it killed her.

Stepping up onto the wooden verandah of the old public house, she felt the very floorboards vibrate. Inside, some group was doing its best to break the sound barrier. And when she strolled through the entrance, with the handsomest guy in Sydney holding her hand, she could see why the building was being rocked off its foundations. There was a frenetic crowd of dancers.

So far, so—great.

In her skintight jeans, heels and clingy top she felt she fitted just fine. Her hair was flowing free. No camellias tucked behind her ear. Nary even a daisy. If she did forget and hum something classical no one would hear. Her nerdiness could go undetected.

She noticed Guy glancing about, scanning the room. As she waited with him in the bar queue, to place their order for pizza, every so often she felt him absently bunch

some of her hair in his hand, then release it. Normally she'd
have given herself over to basking in the sensual chills
and doing her best to surreptitiously bump him with her
behind. Just to give him a thrill. This wasn't that sort of
occasion, though. A different kind of tension was com-
municating itself to her.

When it was their turn to order, the lad behind the bar
was momentarily interrupted by an older barman who
poked his head around and called to Guy.

'Hey, *mate*. Long time, no see.'

Though Guy grinned and lifted his hand in a friendly
gesture, Amber noticed he didn't linger to chat. As soon
as their order was complete he drew her away from the bar
area to find a table in one of the adjoining rooms.

As they scanned for a spot someone else called to him
from across the room, then a couple seated there rose and
made a beeline for Guy.

Guy coolly shook hands with them and introduced
Amber.

Apparently well acquainted with Guy, Jane and Tony
were keen to know everything about how long he and
Amber had been together and how they'd met. Though
Guy was calm, deflecting their questions with smooth
courtesy, the lines of his lean, chiselled face revealed nothing of what he was thinking. An expression Amber recognised with some misgiving.

From the tone of Jane's and Tony's conversation Amber
gathered Guy hadn't been at The Owl for some time. She
could feel the couple's interested gazes switch back and
forth between her and Guy, as if eager to divine every nu-
ance between them.

'And are wedding bells on the agenda here, Guy?' Jane
was at last driven to ask, coyly arching her brows.

Amber felt a bolt of shock at the woman's naked curiosity. Guy's face remained impervious. His only betraying response was the tiny flicker that registered in his grey eyes.

He pulled Amber closer to him, smiled down at her. 'Are you wanting to know every last detail of our relationship, Jane?' he said.

Apparently sensing at last that his partner's curiosity had taken her too far, the husband nudged his wife in the ribs. 'Shh. Don't put them on the spot,' he said, with an uneasy laugh.

After that the couple talked very fast about the beauties of marriage with children, then implored Amber and Guy to join them at their table. Thankfully Guy declined.

As the couple walked away, Amber was still reeling. 'What ghastly people,' she said fervently. 'I'll tell you something, lover, if you ever marry a woman like her I'll never talk to you again.'

Guy glanced sharply at her, then his face relaxed in an amused smile. 'No need to worry about that. I never, ever will.'

After that it seemed every time she and Guy looked around someone would be there, overflowing with friendliness or curiosity or both, and there'd be more handshaking, back slapping. Introductions. Catch-up conversation.

'What are you doing now?'

'Whatever happened to old…?'

'Did you hear I had a new…?'

'Mate, did you catch the Grand Final?'

At one point a bunch of young blokes, some with girlfriends in tow, cornered Guy like a long-lost friend.

'Hey, man, what's goin' down?'

'Man, you wanna hang tomorrow?'

Amber was given the pleasure of meeting the Blue

Suede boys. They welcomed her with wide grins and appreciative glances.

'You do know Amber's my next-door neighbour,' Guy said, his arm around her waist

'Oh, *that* Amber,' one of them said. They grinned at each other, looking a little sheepish.

Laughing, Amber pointed to the beamed roof. 'I hope they've got that screwed down well.'

The Suede pressed her and Guy to join their party, but Guy waved vaguely towards another section of the capacious pub. 'Thanks, but I think we're over there.'

Amber turned to gaze enquiringly at him, but he squeezed her waist.

'Come on,' he murmured in to her ear. 'I'm hungry enough to eat your ear.'

She joined Guy in wishing luck to the boys, then allowed him to hustle her to a table closer to the performance dais. She looked curiously at him. On this side of the room the noise from the band made conversation a struggle. She had to practically shout to be heard. 'Don't you want to sit with your friends?'

'I am. I'm sitting with my girlfriend.'

'Oh, really? Where's she?' She glanced around, as if that mythical creature might be somewhere in the crowd. Secretly, though, she was so madly chuffed she felt herself going pink. She turned back to beam at him, then leaned over and kissed his lips. 'There. That's what girlfriends do. A little something in advance.' She widened her eyes meaningfully and he smiled.

Somehow the food waiter found them. With their feast before them, Guy exhaled a relieved breath.

He began to feel he could maybe relax. Even at the hairy meeting with Jo's cousin, Jane, no one had actually used Jo's name, though he could read the knowledge of his past in some people's eyes. There'd been plenty of assessing glances at Amber, but he'd even noticed people he didn't know checking her out. Who could blame them? What red-blooded guy wouldn't?

All he had to do was make it through the Suede's gig, then he could honourably escort his woman home.

The current band finally finished their last number and vacated the space.

Amber's ears had barely grown accustomed to the blessed respite before a smattering of applause and a few catcalls alerted her to more punishment about to strike.

She glanced up to see the Suede swagger on and start setting up.

One of them stepped forward and introduced the first song, nervously mumbling a few words into the mike she didn't quite catch. Then some heavy opening chords from an electric guitar zithered up her spine with a blood-curdling familiarity she couldn't mistake.

She whipped excitedly around to Guy. 'That's *it*. Your song.'

'Yep.' His eyes gleamed. He listened intently, a small smile curling up his lips, nodding very slightly in time to the beat.

As the song got underway a couple of dancers started gyrating and throwing themselves about. Then several more joined them. Then a whole crowd swarmed onto the floor.

Relieved at last to see the light of pleasure in Guy's eyes, Amber reached to squeeze his hand. 'Look. They love it.'

He returned the squeeze, then urged her to her feet. 'Come on, then. Dance with me.'

To the seriously dedicated dancer a few billion decibels of amplification could actually sound fantastic in the cavernous old Owl, with its high beams and dark-varnished wainscoting. Especially when it came to Guy's song.

Amber could hardly believe she'd scoffed at it. Now, while its emotional, passionate lyrics tore at her very heartstrings, that sexy beat infected her feet with fever. She joined the mass of bodies on the floor and threw herself into the dance with abandon.

When the song finished the crowd roared their appreciation so compellingly the boys in the band played it over.

A little self-conscious to be dancing with a professional, Guy made the minimum moves required by a male—shaking, shuddering, and shifting about from one foot to another. After all his tension, he felt uplifted as much by the thrill of the communal response to his song as by the sheer, joyful, physical exuberance of Amber. Soon they could leave. A few congratulatory drinks with the boys, then he could hardly wait to get her home.

Swinging about to wave to his friends in the band, he received a massive shock.

His heart and lungs froze within him.

At the bar entrance the sight of a familiar red head struck him like a blow. Jo. She must have spotted him at the same time, because he saw her stand still, shock registering on her own face.

Fear.

She turned sharply on her heel to backtrack. Ferocious blood roared to Guy's head. A wild, visceral fury blazed to life inside him, obliterating all other considerations. Oblivious to other people, he fought a path through the crowd. Vengeful words pounded his brain.

He'd make her explain.

He had to make her explain.

Still dancing, Amber was singing, swaying, floating on endorphins when she noticed she and Guy had become separated. Searching for his familiar form among the nearby dancers, she realised he wasn't actually there. Gazing about, her astonished eyes finally located him. He was making for the bar entrance with a grim purposeful stride, seemingly in hard pursuit of someone.

Taken aback, Amber hesitated for a moment or two, wondering whether or not to follow him. Whoever he wanted to talk to, if he'd wanted her along he'd have signalled her, wouldn't he? But, beginning to be jostled by the people whirling and stamping around her, she threaded her way through the crowd and followed in the direction Guy had taken. Through the front of the pub and out onto the verandah.

And stopped.

Her jaw dropped. Guy was in the car park with a woman. In the bright glare of the security lights Amber could see the woman quite well. With a thumping heart, Amber saw she wasn't all that short. She was at least her own height, in fact—maybe even taller—and very sexily dressed in a silky dress, with smooth reddish hair cut in a fabulous sleek bob.

It had to be Jo. Who else?

After her initial shock, Amber could see some bitter words were being exchanged. There was an almost electric fury in Guy's body language. He was doing most of the talking, gesticulating in a style most women would have found intimidating.

Then, to Amber's agonised disbelief, the woman suddenly waved her hands in front of his face, seized Guy's shoulders and kissed him on the mouth.

Hot knives of pain and jealousy sliced Amber's heart to shreds. Clinging to the balustrade for fear of collapsing or imploding, she had no option but to witness the clinch. It wasn't so much that the woman was kissing Guy. It was that Guy wasn't pushing her away. Not at once.

The kiss ended, but Amber saw him hold her fast in his arms as if she was someone rare and precious.

*Then* he pushed her away. Only then.

Seething with hurt and shock, Amber called out hoarsely to him. But he didn't hear. He was far too fascinated by his old love. The woman was talking now, and Guy was questioning her, apparently riveted by her every word.

They turned back towards the pub, still talking. Amber waited for a break when she might attract his attention, but their conversation continued in the same intense, urgent vein.

Totally engrossed. As if they were besotted.

She tried calling out again, though her voice was pretty croaky now. Anyway, if Guy heard her he preferred to ignore distractions like mere girlfriends. With confusion and despair mounting in her heart, Amber couldn't hide from herself the damning evidence of how good they looked together. How right.

The last she saw they were heading into the deserted beer garden at the side of the pub, where tables had been left out under an awning for patrons who preferred a little night-time privacy.

Amber stumbled back inside, her body numb, her heart a crippling ache. Nothing could explain away what she'd witnessed. In pursuit of that woman, Guy had looked as if he was ablaze. If ever passion had existed in him, it was in him then.

She stared unseeing at the scene around her. The noise, the activity left her untouched.

*She'd* seen him looking pretty incandescent. What about that night she'd danced? And last night there'd been passion in him, all right. *And* this morning. And all those other times.

What a monstrous cheek that woman had, anyway, thinking she could just sashay back into his life and snatch him away from his official girlfriend.

The Suede were still belting out songs, but Amber didn't feel like dancing. Not right then.

Instead, operating on instinct, she sashayed up to the bar and asked for a vee juice. The bartender, not a very bright-looking lad, seemed bemused. 'Vodka?'

'Vee,' she rasped, thumping her fist on the bar. 'You know? *Vegetable* juice.'

'Oh. Er…er… Yeah. Hang on…' The guy dashed away and came back with a can of it and a tall glass. 'Any ice in that?'

'No, thanks,' she said shortly, handing over a note. 'I need it fast.'

She didn't bother with the nicety of a straw, just swigged the stuff straight down, lip to rim. Then she checked her reflection in the bar mirror.

Her eyes still had that sultry, sulky look conferred by the shadow. Her neckline still plunged. Good. She whipped out a lipstick and plumped up her pout, good and red to match her toenails, and then, bracing herself, she strode out of the bar entrance and down the steps to the beer garden.

## CHAPTER TWELVE

THE beer garden was enchantingly lit with Chinese lanterns.

At first glance Amber didn't see Guy. Only the woman she felt certain must be Jo. She was seated at a table with her head down. A second glance gave Amber the impression the woman was quietly weeping. Then she saw Guy leaning against the wall by the pub entrance.

Frowning, he had his hands in his pockets and was looking distinctly uncomfortable. Amber wasn't sure what she'd expected to find. Another clinch? Passion in the beer garden?

What she did feel was that she was intruding on something that didn't concern her.

'Oh,' she said uncertainly, preparing to back away.

Guy and the woman both looked up. 'Oh, here she is,' Guy said, suggesting Amber had been the topic of conversation.

Amber nearly goggled. Even with a streaky face the woman was quite stunningly beautiful, with deep, wide-set eyes, fabulous cheekbones and a gorgeous chin. The kind of timeless beauty that cast mere mortal prettiness into the shade. The sort of beauty possessed by the Eustacia Vyes of this world.

Guy detached himself from the wall and strolled over

to slip his arm around Amber. His eagerness to claim her made Amber suspect he viewed her entrance as something of a relief. She had to repress a grin. Weeping women never had been his forte.

'Amber, sweetheart, meet Jo.'

Amber's antennae for emotional disturbance were registering extreme turbulence. Jo's tearwashed gaze did nothing to dispel that impression, although she still managed to give Amber a thorough rival-check.

'Hi, Jo.' Amber took Jo's beautifully manicured hand, noting it felt a little clammy. As well, she had a soggy tissue balled into it, which she tried to palm away, restricting the area available for shaking to a few cold fingers.

'Hi.' Jo looked her over, then applied the tissue to her perfect schnoz, mopped up around the mascara area, and glanced at Guy. 'Trust you, darling,' she said in a wobbly voice. 'You've always had a good eye.'

'Not always,' Guy said at once.

Amber thought she saw Jo flinch.

Guy smiled at Amber then. 'But it might be improving.'

Jo's smile twisted, but she half-lowered her extraordinarily long lashes and said charmingly, 'So. You're a ballerina, I hear?'

'Used to be. Now I'm a florist.'

Guy looked keenly at Amber, narrowing his gaze. Then he said, 'I think it's time we said goodnight, Jo. Amber and I have a big day ahead of us tomorrow.' Then he murmured to Amber, 'We mustn't forget to congratulate the boys.'

Jo had been looking from one to the other of them, a barely perceptible sardonic tug to one side of her voluptuous mouth, but at that she pulled herself gracefully to her feet.

She scattered a few careless farewell words over them, as if walking away from her old love was as much a cinch as strolling down any catwalk. Then, lifting her hand in a backward wave, she undulated on her fabulously long legs out into the car park.

After a few steps, though, she halted. Turned. Undulated back.

As she approached Amber noticed Guy's brows edge closer together. His face hardened and grew stern.

Standing before him once more, Jo made a helpless gesture, all at once sadness and resignation in her lovely eyes. 'You're probably right, darling. I never deserved you. At least now we can give our past a decent burial.'

It was a great exit line. Amber might have felt sorry for her if she hadn't been throwing about the darlings with a frequency that could only be considered indecent. It was such poor taste—especially in front of a man's girlfriend.

Certainly Jo's sadness might be sincere. If it wasn't an act. But there was no doubt in Amber's mind Jo was deliberately and knowingly signalling that she was the woman with the prior claim.

Was she hoping to ease Amber out with her wiles and dramatic exit lines? She needed bringing down to earth.

Amber moved forward a little. 'Is there anything we can do for you, Jo?' she said sympathetically. 'Buy you a pizza? Give you a lift home?'

Jo's eyes clashed with Amber's for a glinting second, then she lifted her brows. 'That won't be possible for you, dear. My home is in Tuscany.'

Then, with a semi-wave, the bewitching woman straightened her shoulders and walked quickly across the car park.

Amber turned to look wonderingly at Guy. '*Does* she live in Tuscany?'

He grimaced and shook his head. 'She might. Who knows?'

'What was that all about?'

'Buy me a drink and I'll tell you. Everything.'

Amber looked closely at him. His eyes gleamed into hers.

'Now, everything, mind,' she said, when they were finally seated in a private little corner Guy happened to know of. *How*, she dreaded to imagine.

At least they were far from the Suede, who were still belting out encores. Drinks were before them. Scotch for Guy, juice for Amber, since she was the one driving home.

She waited for him to start, then urged him into it with a little prompt. 'The last I saw you were racing to catch her like a man possessed.'

'Mmm.' He nodded. 'I know. I'm still reeling. I just can't believe that after all this time I've actually seen her again.'

Amber's heart, still a little rocky after its earlier battering, gave an ominous lurch. 'She clearly means a lot to you.'

'*Meant* a lot,' he said quickly. He lowered his lashes. 'The last I saw of her... Well, I didn't. She didn't show up.'

Amber felt as tense as a wire, questions she didn't care to face forming in the back of her mind. 'Yes, I know. You said she stood you up.'

'That's right.' He met her gaze briefly, a twist of a smile on his mouth. 'In a church. St Andrew's Cathedral, actually.'

The shock rendered her speechless for seconds. Then, as comprehension finally illuminated her brain, she was overwhelmed by the enormity of it.

'You mean you were getting married?'

He shrugged. 'Yep.'

'You asked her to marry you?'

He gave her a resigned look.

'And she stood you up in the church?'

'Yes, she did.'

'But why? Why'd she do it?'

'She told me just now she changed her mind.'

*'What?'* Her voice squeaked in indignation. 'She changed her mind so she just left you *standing there at the altar*?'

'Shh…shh. Don't get excited.' He glanced about. 'You'll have Jane and Tony over to find out what we're up to. But, yeah, that's about the size of it.'

'But—didn't she let you *know*? Why didn't she phone?'

'She couldn't. She was on a plane heading for the Riviera with her old boyfriend.'

'Oh.' The sheer disgrace of the agony and public humiliation that had been inflicted on him brought tears to Amber's eyes. 'I can't believe it. How can anyone be so *selfish*…so *cruel*? No wonder you were… Oh, I see—I see it all…' And she did. Suddenly so much was falling into place. 'Oh, Guy…Guy, you poor, poor man. I…'

She was stroking his shoulder, his back, patting him, touching his face, his hand.

He turned his face away and something dawned on her. He was embarrassed by her emotion on his account. She bit her lip and held off with the words. No one wanted to be reminded of the fool they were once made to feel.

At least when she'd found out the awful truth she'd had that heaven-sent opportunity to pour a pot of beer over Miguel's head.

'Yeah. I think I get it now.' She nodded. 'She probably found out about your weakness for other people's toothbrushes.'

He turned to look at her, then a smile lit his eyes and he broke into a laugh. 'Come here.' Grabbing her, he kissed her lips with a convincing, malt-flavoured fervour that did him credit, considering he'd just bumped into his beautiful ex-bride. Then he said thickly, 'Come on, Amber O'Neill. I want to take you home.'

# CHAPTER THIRTEEN

'MARRIED life's wonderful,' Jean said, beaming at Amber over her champagne and raising her voice a little to be heard above the throng of people crammed into Amber's bunching room. 'I'd never have imagined it could be so much fun. I've known Stuart for years, but the things I've learned since I married him—*well*.'

Amber smiled. Jean certainly did look happy. Her face was so radiant she looked twenty years younger.

It was the Saturday of Amber's grand re-opening as La Primavera. Every inch of the shop not covered in flowers was thronging with people.

'I think it comes of knowing that you don't have to face the big horrors of life alone,' Jean went on. 'And of course *that's* all about finding the right partner. Someone who sincerely cares about you and is on your side.'

'Heavens,' Amber said. 'You're making me all weepy.'

'Oh.' Jean's eyes widened in dismay. 'I'm sorry, dear girl. I don't mean to imply you must be married to be happy. Far from it. I was happy for years as a single woman. I'm just glad I've had this chance to be happy in a new and different way.'

Amber leaned over and kissed her. '*Be* happy, Jean. I'm thrilled for both of you.'

And she *was* thrilled to have Jean back, but it meant

that Guy had collected his belongings and moved over to his own residence at Woollahra.

It had cost Amber more than a small pang to see him move, but he'd said he was keen to be back under his own roof. Amber hadn't seen his house since the renovation stage, but Guy had promised to show her the finished product soon.

'Won't you miss me over there?' she'd said when he was packing his stuff, only half joking.

'I'll make sure I don't,' he said, eyes twinkling. Whatever that meant.

She hated to sound needy. Anyway, she was far too busy to be concerned about it this weekend.

'No need to ask how you got on with my favourite nephew,' Jean continued, giving Amber a guilty start.

For a wild second Amber wondered if she'd left behind some trace of her disgraceful tomfoolery on the piano. She doubted she'd ever be able to drink a cup of tea on Jean's sofa without choking.

But Jean's gentle face was as serene as ever. She smiled warmly at Amber over her glass. 'I doubt if he'd have put so much into your advertising campaign if he didn't think the world of you.'

Amber nodded, smiling. 'We do get on quite well, actually.'

When they had the chance. When he wasn't on the other side of Sydney Harbour.

But she shouldn't complain. The shop's grand re-opening weekend had got off to a splendid start, coinciding with the advertising campaign. Guy had managed to turn the Chinese Garden of Friendship into an Italian painting, and there Amber was, scattering roses on television screens and billboards all over the city.

Best of all was her song—a lyrical little jingle with a

catchy tune the boys in the band belted out with all their might. Now everyone seemed to be singing it. 'Springtime at La Primavera'. What was even more fantastic was that Blue Suede's popularity meant her ad had gone viral.

Amber saw La Primavera below her shamelessly inviting smile everywhere she looked. It had taken some getting used to, not cringing when she saw it. Not to mention being instantly recognisable to large numbers of strangers.

And her Facebook list had exploded.

Friends from the ballet had texted, or written on her wall—including Miguel, of all people. Even others she hadn't been in touch with for ages. Some merely to remind her they were alive, though one of her old instructors had actually begged her to come back to Melbourne and take up the life she was meant for.

That had cost her a pang. As if she really had a choice.

Anyway, her new shop was a delight to the eye.

With the doors open to the street and an abundance of flowers massed inside and out, including an alluring array under her pretty green- and blue-striped awning, the shop was charming. Inside it was like a spring jungle, filled with fascinating little nooks. The boys in the band had painted all the shelves and freshly papered the walls for her, and Serena had painted a beautiful flowery mural of riotous pastels.

Trade had picked up from the very day Serena had started the mural. Since she was working more often than her regular babysitter could accommodate, Amber had suggested Serena bring her baby in to work. Amber wasn't sure if it was the rosebud sleeping in her pram that drew the crowds, or the sight of Serena painting with her newborn cuddling up to her like a koala in her sling, but every day it was becoming necessary to order more and more blooms to keep up with the vigorous demand.

It was only temporary, though. Serena's mother was moving into a flat not far from the arcade tower so she could help Serena more with her babysitting. Soon Serena would be able to work five days.

Ivy hadn't been very comfortable with the changes. She'd felt the open street doors would allow in germs, and for her the baby had been the final straw. Amber had written her a glowing reference and, to everyone's surprise, Ivy had landed a position with Di Delornay.

Amber suspected it suited Ivy to work at Madame because it allowed her to keep an eye on La Primavera without having to put up with Amber's dangerous ideas.

Everyone came to Amber's opening, drank her champagne and bought the charming little bouquets she'd risen at dawn to bunch. Jean and Serena helped to distribute food and help members of the public with their purchases.

Of course Roger from Centre Management dropped by, exuding warm approval of Amber's improvements. Salacious rumours, always doing the rounds in the mall, now had it that at the time of the residents' meeting Roger had been Madame's plaything. Since then, the eager gossips reported, Madame had given Roger his marching orders.

Amber wasn't sure who had started these particular rumours, but she had her suspicions.

Anyway, without an apparent axe to grind *vis-à-vis* tenancy relocations, when Roger met Amber these days he smiled like a congenial uncle. All was forgotten.

Though Guy still didn't like him.

Some of Guy's crew had dropped into Amber's celebrations for a toast, including Kate and Maggie. And naturally the Suede were an item. Besides never missing any sort of party, the boys were on the up and up in the local music scene, and were receiving excellent exposure from Amber's ad.

They rocked in early, skinny in leather and denim, with their hair flopping over their foreheads, and performed Amber's song and several others in the mall before an admiring crowd.

Afterwards they hung around the shop, tossing roses to any attractive young women who happened to stroll by, signing autographs, and eating and drinking anything they could get their hands on.

Most of the arcade tenants found time to come, bringing wine and nibbles and warm congratulations. Some of them were a little sheepish about their part in the pressure applied to Amber to achieve her renovations, especially Marc. He apologised profusely, claiming none of it had been his idea. His excuse was that his strings had been ruthlessly pulled by Madame across the way.

Amber and Serena laughed heartily at this explanation, noting how Marc's dark eyes darted about at all the new fixtures, checking for cracks in the wallpaper. A couple of times Amber caught him staring disconsolately at her gorgeous street entrance.

At the end of the day Ivy accompanied Madame herself for a state visit. Amber was intrigued to notice Ivy had dyed her hair the same coppery colour as Di's, and was wearing one of Di's burnt sienna off-the-rack suits with heels. She'd even had her nails done.

'You look lovely, Ivy,' Amber told her sincerely.

'Oh, well. You have to make an effort to fit in,' Ivy said. 'It never mattered over here. But over *there*…'

Amber lifted her brows and smiled. Poor Ivy couldn't hurt her. No one could.

Everything in her life was rosy. Her shop, her friends, her man.

Although of course he wasn't her man *officially*. And maybe he never would be. A man who'd suffered the trauma Guy had would be unlikely to want to make the sort of commitment most women dreamed about.

It didn't matter to Amber. She could be happy with the way things were. She felt pretty sure they'd still see each other regularly, although it would be a wrench not to wake up beside him every morning.

With the pressures of work for both of them, it wasn't realistic to think she'd see him every day. Though she had been hoping he'd spend a little more time at her party. He had come for an hour this morning, but then he'd had other things to do.

She wasn't worried any more about the Jo situation, of course. Guy had explained a little about Jo's motivations in backing out of the wedding, and he didn't seem to bear any rancour.

'It's a funny thing,' he'd said, leaning up on the pillow beside her one afternoon. 'You know how you read about the scales falling from people's eyes?'

Amber nodded.

'Well, that's how I felt when I talked to her at The Owl. I don't blame her for changing her mind. Anyone should be allowed to draw back—right up until the moment of saying *I do*. It was her explanation for not letting me know that stunned me. She said she was too busy with the preparations for her flight. It was all so sudden, she just didn't think until it was too late.'

Amber was still unable to imagine being in such a hurry as not to remember a waiting bridegroom.

But she was pleased she and Guy had finally talked through the painful experience. Guy had really opened up about the whole thing. Sometimes she had the feeling he'd kept it locked inside for fear she'd in some way hold it against him.

As *if*.

By late on Saturday Amber's energy for the celebrations had begun to flag a little. There were only so many hours of socialising and retailing a woman could do in one day, and she'd been working since before dawn.

'Why don't you go up and have a rest?' Jean had come down again for another bout. 'I'll mind the store for the last hour if you trust me.'

Amber turned to her. 'Oh, Jean, that's a lovely offer. But I couldn't…'

'Yes, you could. Sure you could. Come on. Accept it.' That was Guy's deep voice.

Amber spun around. He'd strolled in, looking dangerously gorgeous and athletic in jeans and leather jacket, his grey eyes gleaming with some barely concealed excitement.

Amber's sharp eye instantly zeroed in on his jaw.

*Aha*. He'd recently shaved.

She narrowed her eyes. 'So, what brings you back here?'

Heedless of his interested aunt and the party crowd, he bent to kiss her lips. 'There's something I want to show you.'

Amber hardly needed persuading. There were infinite ways of relaxing, and she was always open to suggestion.

Once in the car, Guy seized her in a steamy, breath-stealing, wide-ranging clinch that convinced her of his genuine pleasure in seeing her. Then he drove her across the bridge and through the city to nearby Woollahra.

Amber loved the area, with its pretty tree-lined streets and elegant villas. The house Guy had inherited from his grandfather was on the crescent of a hill, with harbour views from its upper storey.

Pulling on the handbrake in the garage, Guy said, 'Come on upstairs.'

The house was built on several levels. Some walls on the garden side had been replaced with glass, to increase the spacious feel of the old residence. There was a faint scent of freshly hewn timber and sawdust.

Amber slipped off her heels so as not to mark the wooden floors.

She felt his eyes on her naked feet and knew at once that their ever-simmering desire was at risk of escalating at any moment. He took her through the sparsely furnished rooms, showing her all his home's beauties of harmony and style. Then on the upper floor he opened a door and stood aside for her to enter first.

She stepped inside and her heart seized. This room was long and wide. As long as the entire house. There was no furniture, apart from a piano at one end, but three of the walls were mirrored and one of them had a *barre* rail. The fourth had wide windows with views of the bay.

'Oh,' she gasped. 'Oh, Guy.'

She walked into the middle of the room, this room that wrenched her heart, hardly knowing what to say. Questions clamoured in her mind. *How come?* she wanted to ask. *Who's it all for?*

*What's the point?*

She turned to look at him, speechless.

He moved towards her, his grey eyes uncertain, even a little anxious. 'You see, I can't believe you're ready to give it up.'

A huge sea of buried emotion somewhere deep inside her welled up and sprang a leak. Tears swam into her eyes. 'Oh, Guy.'

'I thought…correct me if I'm wrong…I thought you

might like to…once the shop is on its feet and thriving…
let someone else run it and take up your career again.'

Why *then* she would never understand, but hearing her
most secret fantasy spoken aloud was too much for the
dam inside her, and whatever had been walling it up so
tightly for so long burst. She covered her face with her
hands and cried.

Guy held her while sobs racked her body and tears
rained on his leather jacket, stroking and soothing her,
patting her and murmuring things like, 'My darling…'
'My beautiful girl…' 'My sweetheart…'

If the poor man was as frightfully embarrassed as she
supposed, he didn't even show it. And when at last she'd
slowed enough to make a hoarse cry of, 'Tissues!' with
urgent pointing motions towards her bag, he rummaged
in its depths and brought out a whole bunch, which she
gladly accepted.

'You do know,' she said, dabbing tissues in all the wet
areas, 'I might not be able to get back into the company?
And my life is here in Sydney now. You. The shop. You.'

'But there are dance companies in Sydney, aren't there?'

She nodded. 'But places here are fiercely contested.
I've been out of it so long I'd have to work like mad even
to reach scratch for an audition.'

'Then that's what you'll do.'

He was so confident for her it gave her such a boost.

Maybe she could do it. She could. If she didn't have to
run the shop full time.

'I've been thinking about your shop. How about letting
Serena run it? She seems to like the business. She could
hire a couple of people to work weekends for her. And you
could let her stay in your flat.'

'But where will I stay?'

He smiled. 'Here.'

Eventually he led her downstairs where, thankfully for her wobbly legs, he had a sitting room with a proper sofa and chairs. Even a thick Persian rug. The plastic covers were still on the sofas, so instead she let her feet sink into the sumptuous pile of the rug.

'The whole place needs furnishing properly,' he said, looking around. 'I thought you might like to have a say in that.'

She lifted her brows. 'Me?'

'Yeah. You see, I was hoping…'

She noted a sudden tension in his stance.

Her pulse made an excited leap and her heart began to bump against the wall of her chest. A throbbing, vibrant tension inhabited the space between them, as if something momentous was about to happen.

He dropped his gaze. 'You know, I never thought I'd trust a woman to love me after what happened.'

'I know.' Her heart ached for him so fiercely she had to apply another tissue to her eyes. 'I'm not surprised. It was a horrible tragedy. No one would get over it easily.'

He shrugged. 'Oh, well… Worse things have happened to people. But when I met *you*… When I saw you for who you are…'

It was hard not to cry when someone was saying such beautiful sincere things. But she willed back the tears, pressed her lips together and held her breath.

His eyes were so warm and tender it was worth the struggle. 'I fell in love with you right away.'

She smiled. 'Did you?'

'Yeah. That day you told me off in the shop. I'm still madly in love with you, if you want to know.'

'I do want to know.' She felt her smile bubbling up inside and pouring through every pore.

'Yeah?' He grinned and kissed her.

She kissed him in return. 'I want to know every single thing.'

He laughed, and she laughed too, though it was pretty shaky, what with her feeling so excited and emotional and her eyes being constantly washed with salt water.

'You know,' she said breathlessly, 'I've been wanting to tell you for so long. About how I love you.'

His eyes glowed. 'Honestly?'

She beamed. 'Honestly and sincerely. With all my heart.'

He took her in his arms and kissed her. It was a deep, fervent and intensely satisfying affirmation. Afterwards they were both breathless, and not a little aroused. He was such a passionate, emotional guy. He always brought out the best in her.

'You know, you're the most beautiful, unique and special woman I ever knew in my life.'

'Truly?' she breathed, hardly able to believe what she was hearing.

'Absolutely,' he said firmly. 'So now I want you to tell me the honest truth about something.' He held her a little away from him and studied her face. 'Honestly, now. Do you want to actually get married?'

He crinkled his brow a little. His crow's feet were charmingly in evidence, somewhere between a frown and a wince.

She hesitated, trying to read his eyes. What if she said the wrong thing here? She could absolutely ruin the moment. But…it was their moment of truth. Would any moment so tender ever come again?

And she knew she just *had* to be true to her inner nerd.

'Well, actually, Guy…' she said, her heart bursting with love and hope. Crossing her fingers, she took a deep breath. 'In actual fact…yes.'

He smiled. Then he laughed. 'Yeah, I thought you'd say that.' He grinned again. 'Great. We'll get married.'

Her heart nearly exploded, her joy was so rapturous. But other sensations were fast asserting themselves—some of them due to that rug and its marvellous feel under her feet.

There was something truly sensuous and voluptuous about a Persian rug.

As her lover kissed her to the floor, thrilling her with the intensity of his desire, she couldn't help sparing a thought for that silly, empty woman who'd thrown away the most gorgeous man on the planet. The most honourable. And the most loving. And very possibly the most virile.

Inspired by the impressive manifestations of his affection, she said huskily, 'Would you like me to show you Straddle Position Number Seven?'

A piercing hot flame lit his eyes. When he spoke his voice was deeper than a subterranean seam of the purest dark chocolate. 'Oh, Amber.' The heartfelt growl in his voice was utterly convincing. 'Sweetheart, you truly are the most bewitching woman alive.'

\* \* \* \* \*

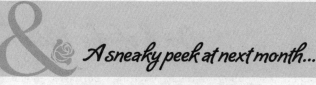

*A sneaky peek at next month...*

# MODERN™

**INTERNATIONAL AFFAIRS, SEDUCTION & PASSION GUARANTEED**

*My wish list for next month's titles...*

In stores from 20th July 2012:

❏ Contract with Consequences – Miranda Lee

❏ The Man She Shouldn't Crave – Lucy Ellis

❏ A Tainted Beauty – Sharon Kendrick

❏ The Dangerous Jacob Wilde – Sandra Marton

In stores from 3rd August 2012:

❏ The Sheikh's Last Gamble – Trish Morey

❏ The Girl He'd Overlooked – Cathy Williams

❏ One Night With The Enemy – Abby Green

❏ His Last Chance at Redemption – Michelle Conder

❏ The Hidden Heart of Rico Rossi – Kate Hardy

**Available at WHSmith, Tesco, Asda, Eason, Amazon and Apple**

*Just can't wait?*

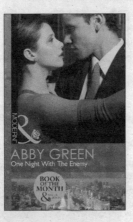

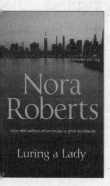